Ca

A Pumpkin Hollow Mystery
by
Kathleen Suzette

Table of Contents

Sign up to receive my newsletter for updates on new releases and sales:

https://www.subscribepage.com/kathleen-suzette

Follow me on Facebook:

https://www.facebook.com/Kathleen-Suzette-Kate-Bell-authors-759206390932120

Chapter One

THE BELL ABOVE THE door jingled, and I looked up from the tray of raspberry truffles I was putting into the display case.

"Mia Jordan," Hazel Martin said, walking up to the display case. She looked me up and down over the top of her silver wire-framed glasses. Her short, curly gray hair sported a pink antique hairpin tucked into the front and her rouged cheeks bloomed under the fluorescent candy store lighting.

"Good morning, Hazel," I said and forced my mouth to curve into a smile. I had moved home a week earlier and Hazel lived next door to my parents. Up until now I had managed to keep from running into her, but my luck had just run out.

"You're just the person I was looking for. I was wondering, is it possible to make the pecan pralines without pecans?" She held her pink rhinestone encrusted purse in front of her, waiting for my answer.

I stared at her for a moment, wondering if this was a trick question. I shook my head slowly. "No. After all, they're pecan pralines."

She sighed and tilted her head. "I detest nuts. They get stuck in my teeth. But I love the pralines themselves. You need to be more mindful of people who don't eat nuts." She looked at me, waiting.

"I'll keep that in mind," I said. I finished putting the rest of the raspberry truffles into the display case and closed the glass door. To say Hazel Martin was a difficult person was an understatement. Next she would be asking me to make chocolate covered cherries without the cherries.

"I want to speak with your mother," she said, brushing invisible lint from the sleeve of her pale pink sweater with one white-gloved hand. It wasn't quite Labor Day and still too warm for a sweater, never mind the 1950s era white gloves.

I smiled and then called over my shoulder, "Mom!"

"How are you doing since you moved back? Your old stomping grounds, eh?" Hazel asked, looking over the candy in the display case. "It's a shame you couldn't make a go of it in the real world. Some people aren't cut out for real jobs, I guess."

I bit my lower lip to keep from saying something I would regret. "Well, you know how it is. The real world is kind of scary." I hoped she would note the sarcasm.

"Indeed it is," she said with a smile.

So much for sarcasm.

My family had lived next door to Hazel since before I was born. I had grown up with her looking over my shoulder, ready to point out any wrongs I had committed. She was a busybody to the nth degree.

"Mom!" I called again. I had work to do and she could deal with Hazel. She was more diplomatic than I was. I sprayed glass cleaner on the front counter and picked up a dry white dishcloth and wiped away the smudges so I wouldn't have to talk to her.

I frowned as I worked, Hazel's words dug in deep. I had moved to Michigan ten years earlier to go to college with a plan to study veterinary science. But taking courses requiring me to dissect frogs, rats, and various other small animals changed my mind in a hurry. I floated through college for two years, finally declaring my major at the end of my sophomore year. English. I loved to read, and I decided I could be a writer or teach at the local junior college with an English major. But after I got my master's degree in English, I worried it wasn't what I really wanted. So I got another master's degree in math. But I wasn't sure about that either, so I got a master's degree in business and web development.

After ten years of higher education and feeling like a spinster where careers were concerned, I moved back home. It occurred to me I might be avoiding the real world by staying in school indefinitely.

Home was Pumpkin Hollow, population 6,353. Pumpkin Hollow was a Halloween-themed town in the mountains of Northern California, far enough from the bigger cities to feel like a proper small town, but not so far as to be inconvenient for tourists. We had nine blocks of shops dedicated to all things Halloween. Around the corner was another street with a haunted house, two Halloween party houses (one for adults and one for children), an old-fashioned roller-skating rink with real hardwood floors, and other various Halloween-themed entertainment. At the edge of town was the haunted farmhouse with a corn maze and straw bale maze.

People came from all over the state to visit, and most importantly, spend their money. The Halloween season, as the locals called it, lasted from Labor Day weekend through about mid-November, depending on where the second weekend landed on the calendar. The remainder of the year saw little more than a trickle of visitors; so planning our business was imperative.

My parents owned the Pumpkin Hollow Candy Shop, passed down from my mother's parents. We sold Halloween-themed candy; some we made, and some we purchased. The rest of the year we sold other holiday-themed candy, but we always carried a variety of Halloween candy, regardless of the time of year.

Hazel peered into the display case while waiting for my mother to appear from the back room. I glanced over my shoulder again and wished she would appear.

"Such a shame to waste your parents' money," Hazel murmured as she bent down and squinted at the chocolate bonbons.

"Mom!" I shouted, looking over my shoulder again in desperation.

"What is it?" Mom asked, coming from the back room, wiping her hands on a dishcloth. She stopped in her tracks. "Oh. Hazel."

"Good morning, Ann. How are you?" Hazel asked. Honey dripped from her tongue, but I wasn't fooled. She was up to something.

"I'm fine, Hazel. How are you?" Mom asked. Her eyes went to me, then back to Hazel.

"I want to take issue with your flag." Hazel clasped her hands together over the strap of her purse. "We need to talk about it."

"What?" Mom asked, looking confused. She untied her apron in the back and took it off, laying it on a stool behind the counter. "What do you mean?"

My mother would try to smooth things over, whatever the issue was, unless she was pushed. And she had spent too many years being pushed by Hazel Martin.

"The flag on your house. The homeowners association forbids flags bigger than 24" by 24", and I'm sure your flag is much too big." She had a smile on her face and I rolled my eyes. How many times had we heard this sort of thing over the years?

"I don't think there's anything wrong with the size of my flag, and I'm sure the homeowners association would have said something by now if there was," Mom said, reaching for a dishcloth to wipe down the counter I had already cleaned. Mom liked to hang decorative flags on the house that she changed out with the seasons. A large flag with a cut watermelon and romping cartoon mice waved from the front porch as we spoke.

"They haven't talked to you about it? I'll be sure and let them know they've overlooked it," Hazel said, nodding. "Now, let's see about these pralines."

I rolled my eyes again. "We aren't changing the recipe for the pralines," I said. "Nor are we changing the flag."

Mom glanced at me, eyebrows raised.

"Mia, the customer is always right," Hazel pointed out. Her glasses were still poised on the end of her nose. As long as I had known Hazel, that's where they sat. I wondered how they stayed put since she was always sticking her nose into other people's business, but I didn't ask.

"Pralines have pecans. That's the way it is," I said, sitting down on the other stool behind the counter. I looked to my mother for support.

"I can't imagine that pralines would be pralines without pecans," Mom said carefully. "Maybe you should try something with a soft center. We have a variety of candies to choose from."

Hazel pursed her lips and shook her head. "I don't understand this. The city council is always telling residents to buy local. Support the town, they say. But then when I try, I run into this resistance," she said, motioning toward me. "I was just over at the Sweet Goblin Bakery and bought a dozen donuts and do you know what Stella Moretti told me?"

I sighed and refrained from asking what Stella Moretti had said. I knew conversations like this would go nowhere. They always did.

When neither of us asked what was said, she continued. "Well, I'll tell you. She said a baker's dozen is twelve donuts and not thirteen! Have you ever heard of anything so nonsensical in your life?" She looked from me to Mom, waiting for a response.

"Well," I finally said. Some days I couldn't keep my mouth shut. "A dozen is twelve."

"No, Mia. I know you younger generation don't know much, college education or not, but a baker's dozen is always thirteen. In the old days, the baker threw in an extra donut or cookie or whatever you were buying, as a good-will gesture. And it's not like Stella was advertising a dozen donuts for nine dollars, either. She was advertising a baker's dozen of donuts. There's a difference."

"Fine, you're right," I relented. And she was right, as much as I hated to admit it. I didn't want to argue. I had stayed up too late the night before and I was tired. I also might have been feeling a little sorry for myself for having moved home. At twenty-eight I was too old to be living with my parents and I really needed to get my own place so I could feel more independent.

"I most certainly am right," she said, smiling like the goose that laid the golden egg. "And now, about those pralines. How soon can you whip me up a dozen without nuts?"

I narrowed my eyes at her. "We are not making pralines without nuts. They come as is. Take them or leave them."

Hazel peered over the top of her glasses again. "Listen here, young lady. I have lived in this town all my life and I will get what I want. Don't you know who I am?"

I paused a moment before answering so I wouldn't say something I would regret. "We are not making pralines without nuts," I repeated calmly, looking her in the eye.

She looked at my mother. "Ann, are you going to make my pralines without nuts?"

Mom shook her head. "No, I'm sorry, Hazel. I don't even know what a praline without nuts would be called. The nuts are the most important ingredient in the candy. They're always made with nuts."

Hazel gasped, her face turning pink. "Well, I never! I'll be talking to the city council about this. They have no business telling the citizens of Pumpkin Hollow to shop local when the businesses are so poorly run."

Hazel slung her purse over her shoulder and stomped out, letting the door swing shut behind her.

I looked over at Mom.

She shrugged. "She's been getting worse. I don't know what's gotten into her. Everywhere I go, someone has something to say about her behavior."

"She's a pushy woman, and I'm tired of her antics," I said. "I don't know how you can stay so calm when dealing with her."

"I know. She's been causing such trouble down at the homeowners association, complaining about everyone. The other neighbors are up in arms about it." She sighed. "Well, I have fudge to make. With nuts." She grinned and headed to the back room.

I sighed. *Welcome home to Pumpkin Hollow.*

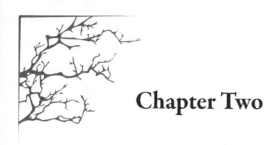

Chapter Two

I looked out the window of my mother's car as we headed home. I have fond memories of growing up in Pumpkin Hollow. I mean, what kid wouldn't love living in a town where Halloween is celebrated year-round? There were Halloween activities every weekend in the fall. Pumpkin-carving contests, kids' Halloween parties at the party house, costume parties during my teen years, and during October, costume contests. On the edge of town, the old haunted farmhouse stood with its two mazes. The corn maze was for teens and adults. It featured villains from horror movies, but it wasn't everyone's cup of tea. The straw maze was simply a maze without any scary characters; kids loved it.

I also remembered trips to the haunted house and hayrides at the haunted farmhouse. I felt tears come to my eyes when I remembered the fun we had. Why had I stayed away so long?

The neighborhood where we lived was neat and clean, kept that way under the watchful eye of the homeowners association. I found it a bit stifling, to tell you the truth. When, or if, I ever bought my own house, I wanted to do as I pleased with it. No one would tell me how to decorate the house I worked so hard to buy.

"You're quiet," Mom said as she turned down our street.

I smiled. "Just a little tired, I guess."

I reached up and pulled the hair tie out of my long brown hair. It was in need of a trim. Maybe I needed to cut it short. I yawned and looked into the rearview mirror. I either needed to get more sleep, or I was looking old for twenty-eight. My eyes were blue like everyone else's in my family and right then, they were accented with dark circles. I had a sister two years younger than me and Hazel had once commented that our parents and the two of us looked so much alike we could be mistaken for quadruplets. Brown hair, blue eyes, upturned noses. I sighed. Hazel needed to keep her mouth shut.

Mom pulled into the driveway and parked the car. The garage housed my sister's furniture and boxes she couldn't find room for after her last move. I wondered when the homeowners association would send a letter to my parents, notifying them they couldn't park a car in their own driveway.

"Glad to be home?" Mom asked, reaching for the door handle.

I smiled and shrugged. "I guess."

"You'll find something," she assured me. "Those college degrees will come in handy."

"Sure," I said and got out of the car. I knew I would find a job. If I could figure out what it was I wanted to do with my life, that is. Every job I had applied for had passed me over and I was beginning to wonder if there was something wrong with me.

Hazel's yard bordered ours. Her flowerbeds were neat and tidy with blooming white mums and maroon zinnias. You'd never catch her yard being out of order. Tools were never left lying around and a garden gnome wouldn't even think about darkening her manicured lawn. The minute a plant died or ceased to bloom, it was ousted and another put in its place. Hazel took her job of beautifying the neighborhood seriously.

I glanced at her front porch. A simple American flag, exactly 24" by 24", hung from a short, skinny flagpole. One potted plant sat near the front door, and a freshly painted white bench sat beneath the front window. I stopped in my tracks.

What was that?

The white painted bench on Hazel's porch had a stuffed scarecrow on it. Even though the town had a Halloween theme, Hazel had never taken part in decorating. For one thing, the homeowners association was strict about what it allowed and its rules had to be kept in mind when shopping for decorations. For another, Hazel didn't like anything fun.

"Are you coming?" Mom asked, looking over her shoulder.

"Yeah," I said, but kept my eye on the scarecrow. Something about it wasn't right. I looked at my mother as she headed to our front door and then back at the scarecrow.

"What are you doing?" Mom asked as she put the key in the lock.

"I'll be right there," I said and walked up the gently mounded grassy knoll that separated our yards.

The scarecrow was life-sized, with one of Hazel's purple gardening hats on its head. Straw poked out from the cuffs of its long sleeves, and its pant legs, and it slumped over a bit. This was definitely against the HOA rules. I mounted the three porch steps, coming to a stop in front of the scarecrow. The oddest part was that it wore the same pink sweater and white gloves Hazel had worn earlier in the day.

"Hazel will yell at you," Mom warned from our porch. "Don't bother her this time of evening."

Something about the scarecrow looked wrong; the way it was slumped over with its head resting on its chest. Why would Hazel put this thing up so early in the year? Why would Hazel put it up at all? Then it occurred to me that someone was playing a joke on her. Hazel, with her super neat yard and the way she looked down on other people's yards, was being pranked.

I breathed out and chuckled. "Someone's going to get in trouble," I said over my shoulder.

I turned back toward my house, stopped, and then turned back to look at the scarecrow again. Hazel would have a fit when she saw it. Not that I cared about her feelings. I reached out and pulled the hat off the scarecrow. It was then I screamed loud enough to wake the dead. All the dead except this one.

Chapter Three

I leaned against my mother's car and watched the EMTs load Hazel onto the gurney and pull the sheet up over her face. I wrapped my arms around myself, looked away, and wondered who could do such a thing. Hazel was a pain, but she didn't deserve this.

There were four police cars parked at the curb in front of Hazel's house and the police milled about the yard and house. One had a camera and busied himself taking pictures. Pumpkin Hollow was a low crime town and the local police had little to do most days. I recognized most of the police, except for the tall blond one.

"Are you okay?" Mom asked, touching my arm.

I nodded and glanced at her, giving her a tight-lipped smile. "I'm fine. Just a little shocked is all."

"I don't know who would do something like this," she said. "Poor Hazel."

"I know. It's terrible."

The neighbors across the street had brought out lawn chairs so they could relax and watch while Hazel was taken away. It didn't surprise me. The Tompkins weren't known for being classy. One year they had placed a mooning wooden mummy cutout in their yard at Halloween. I don't think it was a coincidence that it faced Hazel's house.

Mr. Gott, an elderly widower who lived in the house on the other side of Hazel's house, stood in his yard silently watching the police and EMTs do their job. I sighed. It was a sad night in the neighborhood.

As we stood there, the tall blond police officer looked toward us. He said something to one of the other policemen and headed in our direction. I kept my eyes on him, unsure of what I should do in a situation like this. Everything seemed surreal and I was having trouble taking in what had happened.

"Good evening," the officer said, nodding at my mother and then at me. He smiled. "Mia Jordan?"

I squinted, trying to place him. Then it hit me. "Ethan Banks?"

He nodded and his smile became broader. "It's been a long time."

"It has," I said, stunned that he was standing in front of me in a police uniform. Ethan was taller and had broader shoulders than I remembered. His face had also matured. Gone was the baby face, now replaced by a man's face. A handsome man's face. Not that I noticed.

Ethan and I had gone to school together. With his blond hair, blue eyes and boy-band good looks, he had been the cutest and most popular boy throughout junior high and high school. When he walked by, girls swooned. He was a teenage girl's dream come true. Except for this teenage girl. Ethan Banks had been a bit of a jerk as I recalled. I had never liked him after he teased me about having spiders in my hair in the seventh grade.

It wouldn't have been so bad, but he did it in front of thirty other kids and I spent the rest of the year having kids flip my hair and yell "Spider!" when they walked by. It was traumatizing.

"How have you been?" he asked, his eyes lighting up. "I haven't seen you since graduation."

"I'm good. I've been away to college in Michigan," I answered. I really didn't want to get reacquainted, but I wasn't sure I would have a choice in the matter. I imagined that as a police officer, he would have questions for me about how I found Hazel's body.

"College? Still?" he asked. His brow furrowed in confusion. "It's been ten years since we graduated."

Yeah, I got that all the time.

I shrugged. "Slow learner." It was easier than trying to explain that I still had no idea what I wanted to be when I grew up.

"Oh," he said, nodding. "Did the two of you find the victim?" He was all business now.

I nodded.

"Mia did. I was standing at my door, unlocking it when she screamed," Mom said. "We called 911 right away."

"I see," he said and took a small notebook out of his pocket. "Can you tell me exactly what happened?"

"We had just gotten home from work and I noticed the scare—um, Hazel, on the bench. I mean, I didn't know it was Hazel, but when I walked up to the scarecrow and took its hat off, I realized it was her. And then my mother called 911."

I clenched my hands into fists and my side and wondered if any of that made sense. Why was he making me nervous? He was just Ethan Banks from high school. Except that now he was also a cop and the sight of a police uniform always made me nervous.

"I see. Do you normally check up on your neighbor when you get home from work?"

"What? No, I don't, it's just that it seemed odd she had a scarecrow on her front porch," I said, glancing at the ambulance as it drove off.

Ethan looked up from his notebook. "Why did it seem odd she had a scarecrow on her front porch? I mean, this is a Halloween town and all."

"Are you kidding? Did you know Hazel? She's an obsessive neat freak and she would never have anything like that on her front porch. Was. Was an obsessive neat freak, I mean. And she never decorated for Halloween. Not ever."

Ethan made a note and nodded. "I didn't know her, but I'll admit to taking a few calls for this neighborhood with reports of disturbing the peace and vehicles parked too far away from the curb. The calls originated with her."

"Doesn't surprise me," I said.

"Did you notice anything unusual when you found her? Have there been any strangers in the neighborhood?"

"No, but we work during the day. We haven't noticed anyone new in the neighborhood," I said, and folded my arms across my body.

"What kind of relationship did you have with your neighbor?" he asked without looking up at me.

"What? What do you mean?" I asked.

Was he trying to imply something?

He looked from me to my mom and back. "She seemed like she might not have been the greatest neighbor if she was that picky about things. Did you get along?"

"We got along fine," Mom said. "She complained about things, but we tried our best to ignore her. It was just the way she was and arguing with her wouldn't change things."

"Some neighbors are tough to get along with," Ethan agreed. "You own the candy shop over on Spooky Lane, don't you?"

Mom nodded. "Yes, we've owned it for over thirty years. We inherited it from my parents. We love this town. Pumpkin Hollow is our hometown."

I glanced at Mom. She seemed a little nervous. We both were. The last thing we needed was for the police to think we had something to do with Hazel's death.

"I love the pralines there," he said and smiled. He had a million dollar smile. Not that I noticed things like that.

"With nuts?" I asked. I couldn't help myself. It was out before I realized what I was saying.

"Yeah, the nuts are the best part. Why? Do you make them without nuts?" he asked.

I shook my head. "Nope. Pralines have to have nuts."

Ethan smiled at me like we were sharing an inside joke. I didn't like his friendliness. I wasn't over the spider incident.

"How long have you been back in town?" he asked, sounding chummy again.

"A week." I looked at him without saying anything more. We hadn't been friends in high school. In fact, our paths had rarely crossed. I made sure of that. There was no reason for him to be friendly to me now.

"Are you going to keep working at the candy store? Or put your education to work?"

I narrowed my eyes at him. It wasn't his business what I did with my education. I guess you could say I was too sensitive, but I felt a little like a failure. Each time I had entered a master's program, I had sworn I was on the right track. And now I was back working at my parents' candy shop. I could have saved myself the trouble and money and stayed home.

"I haven't decided. There's an awful lot of people across the street you might want to interview," I said pointing out the neighbors on their lawn chairs.

He glanced across the street and then nodded. "Right. I was just making my way over there. Well, I'll be in touch. If you can think of anything, you'll give me a call, right?" He handed us each a business card.

"Sure," I said without looking at him.

When he left, mom turned to me. "You weren't very friendly to him."

I shrugged. "So? Was I supposed to be?"

"It just seemed odd is all."

I looked at her. "Don't you think he asked pointed questions? I don't like feeling like I'm a suspect in a murder. I was doing a good deed by going over there to check on Hazel."

"Mia, he didn't ask pointed questions and I'm sure all he was doing was trying to find out what happened. He seems like a nice young man." She looked at him as he crossed the street and then turned back to me. "If he did suspect us, and I'm not saying he did, it might be good to be friendlier."

"Mom, he is not a nice young man. In seventh grade, he told everyone I had spiders in my hair. A week later he told them I smelled, and that was why the spiders liked living in my hair."

She looked at me, giving me the eye. "Mia, how long ago was that? In seventh grade, boys are still being mean to girls they like. They don't know how to express themselves."

I gasped. "No, he did not like me. He was just mean. And kids called me 'spider girl' for months afterward."

"I think you need to get over it," she said, turning toward the house. "I'm going to get dinner started. Your father will be home any minute."

I snorted. She didn't know what she was talking about. Ethan Banks was a jerk then, and he was a jerk now. She needed to open her eyes and see what was really going on here.

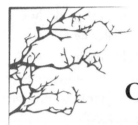

Chapter Four

I WAS PLACING A POUND of caramels into a box for a customer when the shop door swung open.

"Mia!"

I looked up to see Amanda Krigbaum, my best friend from high school. "Amanda!" I said. "Hold on, I'll be right with you."

I took the box of candy to the cash register and rang up my customer. I thanked her and tucked a pumpkin lollipop into the bag for her four-year-old daughter who had spent the last ten minutes eyeing them.

"Come back soon," I said as she left.

"Mia!" Amanda repeated, and came around behind the counter, giving me a hug. "I missed you!"

"I missed you, too," I said. "It's been too long." Amanda looked the same as she had in high school. Tall, blond hair, with piercing green eyes behind black-framed glasses, and a turned-up nose. She was a sight for sore eyes.

"I know. Has it been six years?" she asked, holding me at arm's length. "Let me get a look at you. You're still just as pretty as ever."

"I can say the same about you. I don't know why we let so much time pass without seeing each other," I said. Amanda and I had been inseparable in school. But once school was out, we had gone our separate ways. I went to Michigan, and she went to Texas for college. After college, she moved back home, but her job as a drug sales rep kept her traveling and we kept missing one another when I came home to visit. "How's work?"

"I quit," she said. "I hated all the traveling. I'm engaged, and I didn't want to be away from Brian for long stretches."

I was shocked. "Oh, my gosh," I said. "Congratulations! Brian who?"

"Uh," she said and hesitated. "I'm engaged to Brian Shoate." She tilted her head and looked at me.

I sobered. "Oh. That's great." Brian had been my boyfriend for over a year in high school.

"I'm sorry, Mia. I wanted to tell you, but every time I sat down to call you, I couldn't bring myself to do it. Does it bother you?"

I'll admit I was a little stunned. I shook my head. "No. Not a bit. I'm so happy for you." And I was. It had been a shock when his name came out of her mouth along with the word "engaged", but Brian was a good guy and she was my best friend. They would make a cute couple.

"Are you sure?" she asked.

"Amanda, you're engaged. It's been more than ten years since Brian and I dated. I assure you, I'm fine with it. I'm happy for you." Brian and I had ended our relationship as close to drama-free as two teenagers could make it. Which is to say, there was drama. But it wasn't long after that we were on friendly terms.

She sighed. "I'm so glad. I worried it would hurt your feelings. Brian owns the Little Coffee Shop of Horrors now. I quit my drug rep job and went to work for him. I love being able to spend so much time together."

"Really? I didn't realize he owned the coffee shop. I've been away much too long."

"You have. We've got a ton of catching up to do. What about you? Anyone special in your life?" she asked.

"Nope. I dated a couple of good guys in college, but I'm not seeing anyone right now. Next time I need to tie them up so they can't get away," I said, and picked up a cloth and ran it across the top of the display case. There had been two men in the past ten years that I thought were perfect for me. But things happened, and we parted ways. No drama, no cheating. It just didn't work out. Afterward, I had looked back and regretted letting them go. I didn't seem to be very good at careers or men.

"We may have to do something about that," she said with a grin.

"We'll see about that," I said with a laugh. I was fine on my own. Not that I'd turn down the right guy, but I wasn't unhappy about my single status.

"Hey, I heard your neighbor was killed last night. Was it the nosy one that told your mom when we sneaked out of the house to meet those boys when we were in the ninth grade?" she asked, leaning against the display case.

"That was the one," I said and smiled at the memory. I had lost my phone privileges and been grounded for a month over that incident. "It was weird. Someone dressed her up as a scarecrow and sat her on the bench on her porch."

"That is weird," she agreed. "How did she die?"

"I don't know. It didn't seem obvious when I found her."

"You found her? How horrible!" Her eyes went wide.

I nodded. "It was kind of freaky. I didn't know Ethan Banks was a policeman. He questioned my mom and me about her murder."

"He's been an officer for years. As soon as he was old enough, he went through the police academy. In school I would have sworn he would have become a lawyer," she said.

"I thought so, too. I bet his parents weren't thrilled with that choice. They always seemed like high maintenance people." Ethan Banks lived on the rich side of town in a big house that would fit two of my parents' houses.

She nodded. "They were kind of intense. He was a straight-A student. Law school seemed imminent."

"Do you want to take a break with me? I could use a donut or something," I said. There weren't any customers in the shop and now was a good time to get something to eat.

"Sure," she said. "I'm always up for a donut."

"Mom, I'm going down the street for a donut. I'll be back," I called to my mother.

"Okay," she said and stood in the doorway to the kitchen. "Hi, Amanda."

"Hi, Mrs. Jordan."

We headed out the door and down the street toward the bakery. The great thing about a small town is that most things are within walking distance.

"Hazel was in the shop yesterday morning and she said she'd had an argument with Stella Moretti at the bakery," I said as we walked. The bakery was famous for its chocolate donuts with orange icing and Halloween cutout sugar cookies. Stella Moretti could be a pain to deal with, but she made the best donuts in the county.

"I'd bet Hazel had lots of arguments with almost everyone in town," she said. "I'd be amazed if there was anyone she overlooked."

"That's true," I said with a chuckle. "It's kind of scary having a murderer on the loose though."

She nodded. "I hope they find the killer soon."

I pushed open the bakery door and the scent of sweet yummy donuts hit me. I inhaled. "Hi, Stella," I said. She was behind the counter, sitting on a stool and reading the newspaper.

"Hey," she said, glancing at us, then went back to her reading. Stella was middle-aged with short dark curly hair. She was what my grandmother would call pleasingly plump, and she wore bright red lipstick every day.

We looked over the donuts in the display case and waited for Stella to ask us what we wanted. Stella folded over the newspaper she was reading without looking at us again.

"Stella, can we get some donuts, please?" I asked when she didn't get up.

She sighed loudly. "Sure," she said, folding the newspaper in half again and slowly getting to her feet. She laid the newspaper on the stool and stepped up to the counter.

"Did you hear what happened yesterday?" I asked her.

"What? About that Hazel Martin?" she snorted. "Good riddance. She was a pest. She was always coming in here and arguing about how many donuts are in a dozen."

"It's a shame though," I said. "Ending up dead like that and then being used as a Halloween prop."

She went to the sink on the wall and turned the water on. "Yeah, sure. But it's not like the town is losing anything. She lived to make people's lives miserable. Who's going to miss that?"

I glanced at Amanda.

"She was still a person, Stella," Amanda pointed out. "You have to feel bad about her murder on that basis alone."

"No, I really don't," Stella said, shutting the faucet off and grabbing a paper towel to dry her hands with. "What do you want?"

"Three of the chocolate and orange ones," I said. "I'll bring one back to my mother. She loves your donuts."

"You know what I think?" Stella asked, pulling a square of waxed paper from the dispenser.

"What?" I replied.

She pulled two more waxed paper squares from the dispenser before continuing. "Hazel's killer should be celebrated. We should put up a stone monument dedicated to him or her." She slipped some vinyl gloves onto her hands and went to the display case.

"That's terrible. How can you say that?" Amanda asked. Her eyes went wide, and she looked at me. "How can she say that?"

"She complained about me to the health department. She said I wasn't washing my hands before serving people. You just saw me do it, didn't you?"

"Yes, we did," I said, nodding. "And since your customers know you wash your hands, her complaints are untrue, and I'm sure the health department will figure that out." Hazel was difficult, no argument there. But saying her killer should be celebrated was a bit much.

"Stupid woman," she said, shaking her head. "I am impeccably clean. My shop is impeccably clean. She hated that I collect garden gnomes. She said they were trashy." She looked at Amanda and then me. "Garden gnomes are not trashy. They're cute. I don't know what her problem was, but she kept turning me in to the homeowners association."

"She had a thing for neat yards," I said. "And she turned a lot of people in to the homeowners association."

Stella lived three blocks away from my parent's house and it was true about the gnomes. She probably had more than twenty of the colorful little creatures on her porch and along her fence line. Sometimes the grass wasn't cut, and the house needed a coat of paint, but I had never thought Stella was dirty. Hazel had impossible standards.

Stella rang up the donuts and put them in a white paper bag.

"Thanks, Stella," I said and took the bag from her.

"Tell your mom I said hi. And tell her to let me know when she makes the pumpkin spice fudge again. I love that stuff."

"I will," I said as we left the bakery. After Labor Day, all the shops would have pumpkin flavored everything. I loved pumpkin spice, but I wasn't sure about the pumpkin burgers that Diner of the Dead served. The burgers had pumpkin butter on them. That was going a little too far for my tastes.

"Stella sure isn't going to miss Hazel," Amanda said as we walked down the street. Most of the shops had Halloween characters, pumpkins, and fall leaves painted on the borders of their windows, ready for the start of the season. They had also set their best decorations and merchandise in displays in their front windows. It made me feel nostalgic and giddy with anticipation. I handed Amanda a donut and took one out for myself.

"No, there's no love lost between Stella and Hazel. I don't know how she could be so cold about it though. I know what a pain Hazel was; I lived next door to her all my life. But I still feel bad she died."

"And in such a bizarre manner. Who would dress her up as a scarecrow?" She took a bite of her donut and nodded. "This is the nest donut ever."

"Someone with a terrible sense of humor. And you know, I don't like that Ethan Banks is looking in my direction as a possible killer. He might be looking at my mom, too."

"Do you really think he is?" she asked.

"It sure seems that way," I said and took a bite of my donut.

"I don't blame you for worrying about it, then," Amanda said and took another bite of her donut.

"Maybe I'm jumping to conclusions. I don't know."

I did wonder if my mother and I were really suspects, or if Ethan was just doing his job. Maybe he asked everyone the kinds of questions he had asked us. It was when he asked if we got along with Hazel that bothered me the most. I could have been a little paranoid. I just didn't know for sure.

Chapter Five

"STELLA WANTS TO BE notified when you make the pumpkin spice fudge," I said to my mother and handed her the bag with the last donut.

Amanda had work to do and had gone back to the coffee shop. I was glad she had stopped in. Since moving back to Pumpkin hollow, I had made myself scarce, too embarrassed about having to move home to my parents' house to face anyone. It was good to see an old friend though, and Amanda had managed to make me feel better about being home.

"Labor Day weekend. She already knows that," Mom said, peering into the bag.

"She isn't the least bit sorry about Hazel being murdered." I sat on a stool behind the counter. "I guess I shouldn't be surprised."

"That doesn't surprise me a bit. Those two hated each other," she said and took a bite of her donut. She climbed up on the other stool behind the counter to sit and enjoy it.

I turned to look at her. "Hate is a strong word," I pointed out.

"It's an accurate word. Hazel had an affair with Stella's husband over thirty years ago."

"What?" I exclaimed louder than I intended. "What do you mean she had an affair with Stella's husband?"

She nodded. "Hazel was a looker back in the day. And she had a thing for Vince Moretti. Hazel's own husband was away on business a lot and she got lonely, I guess."

"That is crazy. I would never have thought it," I said, trying to picture Hazel being both younger and a looker.

Mom took another bite of her donut. "This is so fresh," she said. "You can't blame Stella for hating Hazel all these years. Rumor has it she walked in on them."

"Wow. Do you think Stella could have murdered Hazel?"

"I don't see why she would. It's been so many years. If she were going to do it, she would have done it long ago."

"What if all those years just compounded the anger and feelings of betrayal?" I pointed out. "Maybe she lost her mind and snapped after obsessively thinking about it for so many years."

"Maybe. But I think your imagination is running away with you. I don't think anger works that way. If she were going to murder Hazel, she would have done it in a fit of rage when she first found out about the affair. Instead, she stayed married to Vince all these years and Hazel went on with her life."

"Maybe," I said, thinking it over. I wasn't completely convinced.

"I think it would be a good idea to hire some part-time help through the Halloween season," she said after we sat in silence a few minutes. "I've talked to your father and he thinks it's a good idea."

"Really?" I asked. We'd always had part-time help over the years, but the last two employees we'd had moved on over a year ago, and Mom never replaced them. She had been trying to run the candy store by herself with my sister helping out when she could, and Dad helping on the weekends. But my sister had moved away nine months earlier and had recently returned to Pumpkin Hollow, too.

She nodded. "The Halloween season wears me out anymore."

"I think it's a good idea. You work too hard. I don't know how you've managed things almost completely by yourself."

She sighed. "I do what I can."

The door swung open, and I looked up to see Ethan standing there. He smiled at me like we were old friends and I had to keep myself from glaring at him. The spider incident wouldn't be soon forgotten.

"Hi Mia, Mrs. Jordan," he said. "How are you ladies doing today?" He walked up to the front counter in his uniform, looking for all the world like the handsome young policeman he was. I shook my head at the thought.

"Fine," I said but didn't return his smile. He could save it for someone that cared.

"I'm doing well," my mother said. "How are you?"

"Good, thanks for asking," he said and looked at me.

I picked up the morning paper and folded it over.

He leaned against the display case and looked over the candy. "What are those?" he asked, pointing to the display case.

"Almond nougats. They're very good if you like almonds," Mom said, and took another bite of her donut.

"I do like almonds," he said and then he looked at me. "So, how are you doing today, Mia?"

"Great," I said and refrained from pointing out he had already asked.

He nodded and we stared at each other.

"So, that was weird. What happened to Hazel, I mean," he finally said.

"Yes, it was. Did anyone know anything about what happened?" I asked, trying to sound casual.

He shook his head. "No. No one seemed to know anything, and they didn't seem to mind all that much that she was killed. It's kind of sad, if you ask me."

"What about her family?" I asked. "They had to care."

"We're trying to contact them," he said. "Do you know if she had any family in town?"

"She has a sister in Vermont, but all her family that used to live here in town has moved or passed away," Mom supplied. "When her husband died, her in-laws left town and I don't think she ever heard from them again. It's very sad, but she didn't seem to have many friends in this town—not that she ever tried to be friendly. I don't know why she stayed."

"Do you have contact information for her sister?" he asked.

Mom shook her head. "No. But her sister's name is Mary Ann Gould, and she lives in Montpelier, Vermont. Maybe you can Google her."

"That will help. I can start there," he said and took his notebook out and wrote down the name.

"I've got bonbons to make. Let me know if you need anything else," she said, slipping down off the stool and heading for the back room, leaving me alone with Ethan. I gritted my teeth and looked at her for help, but her back was to me.

"Do you make all of the candy you sell?" he asked, smiling at me.

"We make most of it, but we do buy some prepackaged candy from suppliers. And I can make just about any of the handmade candy, but mom enjoys it, so she ends up making most of it," I said, and looked away from his steady gaze.

"It must have been a kid's dream to be raised with the family business being a candy shop," he said.

"I do have a fair number of fillings in my teeth to prove that the family business is operating a candy store," I said with a smile I couldn't hold back.

Ethan had filled out in a good way since high school. Even though he had been the most popular boy in school, I had always thought him a bit on the skinny side. He wasn't skinny anymore.

"Mia, I'm sorry if I came on too strong last night. I didn't mean to. I was just trying to find out as much information as I could."

I shrugged. "No, not at all. I understand, it's your job." I was feeling a little kinder toward him, and I shook myself. I didn't want to feel kindly toward him. I didn't need a man in my life and certainly not this one.

"Good. I wouldn't want you to think I was targeting you or anything. Will you be at the city council meeting tomorrow night?" he asked.

"What city council meeting?"

"They're having one tomorrow to discuss the future of the Halloween season. Business hasn't been what it used to be and some town residents want to do away with it."

I gasped. "Are you kidding? How come I don't know anything about this? They can't do away with it! It's our heritage. It's what makes this town special."

"I know what you mean, I'd hate to see it happen. It's all I've ever known." He sounded sad when he said it.

"Businesses depend on the Halloween season and all the tourists that come to town. We need that money," I said. I couldn't imagine Pumpkin Hollow not having all the Halloween themed shops, the haunted farm, and the haunted house.

"I was pretty shocked when I heard about it, too. It would be a shame if we lost it all."

"What will the town do to bring in more revenue if it's gone? I get that we don't do a lot of business in the off months, but from Labor Day weekend through mid-November, everything Halloween themed brings in a lot of tax dollars for the city. Whose idea was this?" I asked.

I was outraged. Pumpkin Hollow's Halloween theme began in the fall of 1946. Soldiers had come home from the war and the women that had taken over their jobs in their absence were laid off. Another source of income was needed by the families and someone had come up with the Halloween season. The Halloween season had thrived and had been a mainstay of our community ever since.

"It was the mayor's idea," he said, frowning. "To be honest, I am not a fan of his."

"Well as of right now, neither am I."

I looked out the window as a mother and small boy walked past. The boy looked to be about three and he held the string to an orange balloon. The mother pointed to something across the street and the boy stopped to look, losing his grip on the balloon. The balloon floated off into the blue sky.

I looked at Ethan, biting my lip in thought.

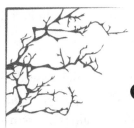

Chapter Six

THE TOWN HALL CENTER was nearly filled as I slipped into a seat in a middle row. I was hoping most of the people here supported keeping the Halloween season. I couldn't imagine what the town would be like without it.

I glanced around and near the front I saw Stella Moretti and Polly Givens from the gift shop. Ethan leaned against a wall, still in uniform, along with his partner Jasper Smith. I sat back in my chair and waited while the secretary read the minutes of the last meeting. New curbs were needed along Third Street, trash pickup was needed an extra day each week, and there were dog licensing concerns. I yawned.

When that was finished, someone I didn't recognize raised his hand and entered an initiative to abandon the town's Halloween theme. A murmur went up in the room and I wasn't sure if it was in support or against the idea.

Stan Goodall, the mayor, raised a hand to quiet the crowd. Stan was middle-aged with a balding head and a slight potbelly. He had been a math teacher at the high school but had quit amid a scandal involving the Glee Club and candy sale money that was never accounted for. It made me wonder how he had ever been elected mayor.

He turned to the man that had raised the motion. "Mr. Crownover, what are your reasons for Pumpkin Hollow to cease being a year-round Halloween themed town?"

"Mr. Mayor," Mr. Crownover said. He got to his feet and took himself by the lapels. "In light of the recent death of an esteemed citizen, I feel it's necessary to examine how we conduct ourselves. Tourist numbers have been down in recent years and with this murder, we can only expect things to get worse."

At the words "esteemed citizen" there was another murmur in the room. I was as surprised as anyone to hear Hazel referred to in that way, considering nearly everyone disliked her.

The mayor put a hand up to quiet the crowd again. "Continue," he said to Mr. Crownover.

He sighed. "Mr. Mayor, we're a laughingstock. We've been one for years. We don't have the resources to continue holding the activities for the Halloween season and now we have a murderer on the loose who is dressing his victims as Halloween props. I vote we immediately terminate everything Halloween."

"Terminate Halloween?" Fagan Branigan said, jumping to his feet. His shock of red hair bounced in the air. Fagan owned the Little Shop of Costumes three doors down from our candy shop. "We can't terminate Halloween. Pumpkin Hollow has been a tourist town for decades. We can't just stop everything Halloween!"

"Fagan, you don't have the floor," the mayor pointed out. "Please sit down until it's your turn."

"I'll sit down, but I won't allow this 'terminate Halloween' idea to go forward. I'll tell you that much." Fagan sat down, folding his arms across his chest, and I smiled. There was at least one other person in favor of keeping the Halloween season alive.

"Mr. Mayor, as I was saying," Mr. Crownover said. "We're a laughingstock. The buildings are in disrepair, the carousel doesn't work, and last year one of the goats from the petting zoo stole over forty personal items from guests. We had complaints all season long. We no longer make money from Halloween. The city has had to maintain the decorations downtown, and replaced them so many times, they've lost count. That money would be better spent on other things."

The mayor nodded. "I have to agree with you. The city doesn't have the money for these types of expenses and with the Halloween season just days away, I don't see how we can go forward."

There was an audible gasp in the room. I looked around and spotted Stella Moretti three rows up, nodding her head. I knew she was a grouch when it came to Halloween, but I hadn't thought she would agree with the mayor. She had a bakery in the Halloween district, after all.

Brian Shoate sat in the row ahead of me and he glanced over his shoulder. We made eye contact for a second, and then I looked away. I didn't have issues with Brian, but suddenly I felt a little weird that he was marrying my best friend.

Fagan stood up again. "Is it my turn now?"

The mayor sighed and rolled his eyes. "I suppose so."

Fagan stood up to his full height of six-feet. "We have a tradition to uphold here in Pumpkin Hollow. My parents and my grandparents owned businesses here. And that talk about us being a laughingstock is hogwash. People look forward to visiting our town. Time and again, I've had customers tell me they've been coming every year since they were children. Even the ones that come in the off-season are thrilled to stop in the shops and visit with the shop owners. And spend their money, I might add. We cannot get rid of the Halloween theme of this town. I'd also like to point out that the murderer doesn't have 'victims,' he or she has one victim. As far as we know, anyway. We shouldn't blow things out of proportion."

"Is that all?" the mayor asked, barely containing his ire.

I wanted to stand up, but I wasn't great at public speaking. Fagan looked around for support, but when none came, he sat down.

Mark Somers stood. "I'd like to add something. Personally, I don't mind the Halloween theme, but it's costing the city too much money to maintain. I vote we shut it down. It's nothing personal. We just can't afford it. We don't have nearly as many visitors year-round as we used to. It's time to hang it up."

I rolled my eyes. Mark Somers only lived in town during the summer and fall. He spent winter and spring in San Diego because he couldn't stand snow. He wouldn't know how many visitors we had during the year because he wasn't here all year long.

"Thank you, Mark. Does anyone else have anything to add?" the mayor asked, looking around the audience.

Mr. Gott, the neighbor that lived on the other side of Hazel, stood.

"Yes, Mr. Gott?" the mayor asked.

"I vote in favor of ending the Halloween season. I'm tired of kids running across my lawn and I have to dodge them in the street when driving my car. It's dangerous having so many kids running around town. Also, inviting strangers to come to your town is just plain dangerous. We don't know who these people are and there's no telling what they might do. Case in point—Hazel Martin is dead. But most of all, this Halloween season is just plain silly. We need to end it right away."

I sighed loudly. Did Mr. Gott really think that if we got rid of the Halloween season, the kids would leave town?

"Thank you, Mr. Gott," the mayor said and looked around for more supporters.

Three more people stood up to support ending the Halloween season, and I was starting to worry. How could so many people be against it? It was what made our town unique. If we abandoned the Halloween season, would we also abandon the name Pumpkin Hollow? Before the first Halloween season back in the 1940s, the town had been named Pine Tree. Who wanted that name back? It was boring.

When no one else got to their feet to support the season, I decided I couldn't sit there without saying anything. I stood.

"I'd like to say something." I paused and looked around the room. "There aren't any other towns in the state like Pumpkin Hollow. There probably aren't any other towns like Pumpkin Hollow in the whole country. People come from all over the state to visit, and it's a tradition for many families. Maybe we don't have the tourist draw we used to have, but maybe we can change that. Maybe we can put our heads together and come up with a plan to save the town." I looked around and saw a sea of eyes staring back. My stomach heaved.

The mayor squinted at me. "Who are you?"

I cleared my throat. "Mia Jordan. My parents own the Pumpkin Hollow Candy Store. My grandparents owned it before that."

"Why haven't I seen you around?" the judge asked, scrutinizing me.

"I've been away to college. For a while. And besides, I had you for tenth-grade math, so I don't know why you don't recognize me."

He studied me a moment longer before speaking. "Well, Miss Jordan, let me tell you, if you've been away for any length of time, this town has changed. It's not the old Pumpkin Hollow you might remember. We don't have the guests we once had, and we don't have the tax revenue we once had, either."

"Are we utilizing the Internet to draw people in?" I asked, sticking my chin out. I wasn't going to give up that easily.

He stared at me again, and then blinked. "We have the Internet if that's what you're asking. And it works fine."

I heard a couple of snickers. "Yes, but do we have a city website that people can visit when they plan their trip? Are we advertising? Are we making the website interactive?"

He sighed. "That all costs money, and if you had been listening, you'd know we don't have money."

"Maybe we can come up with a way to do it at a lower cost. Maybe we can figure out some new ways of doing things," I suggested. I looked around for support, but I felt a little like

Fagan must have felt a few minutes earlier. There were blank stares and frowns on the people around me.

"We don't have the resources," the mayor said. "The Halloween season has outlived its usefulness."

"You can't just end the Halloween season because a couple of people don't want it," I pointed out.

The mayor frowned and narrowed his eyes at me. "It's a waste of time and money to entertain keeping the Halloween season."

"Wait a minute. We can't just end the Halloween season like that. Don't the business owners have a say in things?" Ethan asked, standing to his feet. "It seems like it will affect the business owners the most."

The mayor sighed and rolled his eyes. "The business people may vote. But, it's not like they can't keep their businesses running. If the vote passes, we'll simply abandon the Halloween theme. People still buy candy, even if it isn't pumpkin shaped."

"I can't keep my business going if there's no Halloween theme," Fagan pointed out. "I sell costumes. Halloween costumes."

"And do you sell them year round?" the mayor asked.

Fagan nodded. "It might surprise you, but I do. I also sell online, but I need the local business during the Halloween season to make a living."

"I suppose we might need to take a vote," the mayor said uncertainly.

"We need to do that at the very least," Fagan said. "We have a right to be heard."

"Like I said," the mayor intoned. "We'll take a vote at our next meeting. This meeting is adjourned." He slammed the gavel on his desk before anyone else could speak up and then tossed it to the side and stood up. He glared at me and left the room.

Ethan turned and looked at me. We needed to come up with a plan.

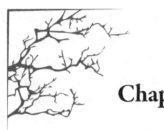

Chapter Seven

I STOOD IN FRONT OF Little Coffee Shop of Horrors trying to get my courage up to go inside. It wasn't that I had feelings for my ex-boyfriend, Brian. I was happy for Amanda and Brian. I wasn't sure what it was, but it had felt odd to see him the night before. He left right after the meeting and I never got to speak to him. I took a deep breath and pushed the door open.

Brian was standing at the front counter, finishing up with a customer. He looked up and smiled when he saw me.

"Hey, Mia, how are you?" he asked as his customer picked up her cup of coffee and headed for the door.

I forced myself to smile and told myself there was nothing awkward about this. "Hi Brian, I'm good. How are you?"

"Great," he said. We stood and looked at each other for a moment. "It's good to see you. Amanda told me you moved home."

I walked up to the counter. "Yeah, I guess it was time. It's good to see you, too. I think I need a coffee. I can't seem to get going this morning." I looked over the chalkboard menu on the wall. "Choco Boo Berry sounds interesting." I tried not to notice that his shoulders were broader than they had been the last time I saw him and the freckles had faded from his nose.

"That's a raspberry mocha, and it's fantastic if I do say so myself."

"I'll have a medium, then. Amanda told me you two were engaged. Congratulations."

He grinned at me and made my coffee. "Thanks. I've never been happier."

I paused. "That's great to hear. How's business been?" I asked. His eyes seemed bluer than I remembered, and his black hair had a single gray hair on the left side of his head.

"Not bad. I still see plenty of customers, regardless of what other people say about business in town. I can't wait for the Halloween season. I'm sure things will be even better then. It always is."

"Yeah, I'm a little worried about what happened at the town council meeting last night," I said, glancing around the empty shop. "Do you think they might really do away with the Halloween season?"

His face sobered. "I hope not. It's what makes this town what it is. I'd hate to see it go. But I can tell you from being a town council member in the past, a lot of things get brought before the board that never pan out."

"I hope that's true in this case. A lot of people earn their livelihood from the Halloween theme."

"We both know how we'll vote when the time comes. Lots of people have ideas of their own but they never follow them through," he said and squirted whipped cream on my drink. "Let's hope this is one of them."

"Oh," I said, and then stopped.

"Sorry. Did you not want whipped cream? I can make you another."

"No, it's fine. I should have said something."

"Sorry," he said and handed me the coffee.

"It's not a problem." I pulled my debit card out of my pocket to pay for the drink.

"It's on the house," he said. "It's been forever since I've seen you. We'll call it a welcome home gift."

"Thanks, Brian, that's nice of you. Where's Amanda?"

"She had errands to run. She'll be in later."

I nodded. "I guess I better get going then," I said. I started to turn and head out the door, but I stopped. "Brian, did you know Hazel Martin? Other than from when we were kids and you would come by my house?"

"Sure, she came in nearly every day and complained I made the coffee too strong. I suggested she add more cream, but that didn't seem to appease her. It's a shame someone killed her."

"It was horrible what they did to her. Who would dress her as a scarecrow like that?" I wondered.

"It seems like an in-your-face act, doesn't it? I hope the town doesn't get bad press because of it. We've always been family friendly and it might drive people away," he said, leaning on the front counter.

I nodded, and the door opened. We both turned to see Ethan and his partner, Jasper, walk in.

"Hey," Ethan said, looking at me, and then over at Brian.

"Hey," I said.

"How are you, Mia?" he asked before I could make my exit.

I smiled. "I'm good. I probably should get back to the candy shop though. I hate leaving my mom by herself for long."

He nodded, but he was blocking the door and made no move to let me by. "I'm glad you spoke up at the meeting last night. It's ridiculous that they're using Hazel's murder as part of the reason to shut down the Halloween season. I mean, it's a terrible thing that happened, but it doesn't make sense they want to stop the Halloween season because of it," Ethan said.

"I know, I just don't understand. It sounds like they're jumping to conclusions."

"What it is, is the mayor having a stake in reelection," Jasper said. "He has people breathing down his neck about making changes, and he wants to get votes, so he's doing what they want."

"Well, those of us that want things to stay the same vote, too," I pointed out. "And who is that Mr. Crownover, and why did he suggest we end the Halloween season?"

"That would be the mayor's brother-in-law," Jasper said. "He's lived here about two years, I think. Notice that the mayor didn't point their relationship out?"

I groaned. "He has no stake in this town, then. It's none of his business what we do here."

"Maybe the mayor thinks people that don't like the Halloween season outnumber those that do," Brian said from behind the counter. "He's going to try to stir them up and get them to vote to end it."

I sighed and took a sip of my coffee. "So many families depend on the Halloween season. It's unfair to try to take that away from them."

"What about a website, like you mentioned?" Ethan asked me. "Do you know how to build a really nice one? I can build a very simplified website, but I know there's more to it to make it successful. Do you think it can be done without spending a lot of money?"

I smiled. I might finally be able to put part of my college education to work. "I think I might be able to help with that. I have a master's degree in web and business development."

Ethan grinned. "Sounds like you came home at just the right time."

"I'll say," Brian said.

Maybe I really had come home at just the right time. And maybe all that studying hadn't been in vain. I wasn't sure I could save the town, but if there was a chance, I was going to give it my all.

"I'll create a website. Driving business to it will take some effort and I'll need help from all of you. Maybe we can save Halloween for Pumpkin Hollow."

"Sounds like a great idea," Brian said. "I know Amanda and I would be grateful. I hate to see people try to run small businesses into the ground. We have rights, too."

I nodded. "My mom and dad would be devastated. They inherited the candy store from my grandparents. I have a lot of old black and white pictures of my grandparents when they were young and working in the candy store. We still have the original display case from when the store first opened. I should blow up some of those pictures and frame them. They'd look awesome on the wall of the candy store."

"That would be very cool," Ethan said.

"Well, I better get back to work. I'll talk to you all later," I said and headed to the door.

I HAD A GREAT IDEA while experimenting with a pumpkin truffle recipe earlier in the day. If all the business owners with a Halloween theme banded together, we might be able to convince the city council how much we needed the Halloween season.

That evening, I sat on my bed with my laptop and created a flyer inviting business owners as well as interested citizens to an impromptu meeting Friday evening. I made it cute with pumpkins and bats bordering the page. I was going for an urgent call to action message, but I hoped it didn't sound desperate. The last thing I wanted was for people to feel like we didn't have a chance of winning.

When I was satisfied, I sent the flyers to my printer. I was going to hand out as many flyers as I could and post them all over town. An ad in the newspaper and posting all over social media was also on the agenda.

Maybe if we all worked at it, we really could save the Halloween season, and in turn, Pumpkin Hollow.

Chapter Eight

I WAS SCOOPING ORANGE and black candy dots out of a box and putting them into the display case when Martha Mayes came into the candy store.

"Good morning, Mia," she said. "My grandchildren are visiting this weekend and I want to get some taffy."

I smiled. "Good morning, Martha. We just got some in," I said, motioning toward a bulk bin.

Martha went to the bin and picked up one of the Halloween print paper bags that sat below the bin. We had just gotten in a fresh supply of the bags. During the off-season, we used white paper bags, but with Labor Day less than a week away, we were gearing up for the Halloween season.

"These sure are good," she said, scooping some of the multi-colored taffy into her bag.

"Yes, they are," I said and closed the display case. "My mother said she's going to make vanilla taffy in the next few days. The store-bought taffy is good, but you don't want to miss the handmade taffy."

"I'll have to stop back by and get some of the vanilla taffy when she makes it, then. Mia, I was sure sorry to hear it was you that found Hazel the other day," she said, closing the lid to the bulk taffy bin and folding over the top of the paper bag. "What an awful thing to see."

"It was rather unpleasant," I said, picking up a box from the floor and opening it. Inside were two-dozen orange and black votive candles I was going to set around the shop to help with the Halloween ambiance. "I feel bad for Hazel. I haven't heard if they know how she died. Have you?"

"No, not a word. I don't feel especially bad about her dying though. You have no idea how many calls I got from her each week." She walked up to the counter and put the bag down. Martha was the manager of the homeowners association for my parents' neighborhood and was in charge of making sure everyone complied with the rules.

"You don't mean that," I said. I knew Hazel was a pest, but it was beyond me how anyone could say they didn't feel bad about someone's murder.

"Actually, I do. I tell you, Mia, she was something else. She had laser vision and the minute someone's grass was more than a half an inch too high I got a call. And heaven forbid someone had a garden gnome in their front yard. That Stella Moretti was at the top of her list to complain about, but you and your parents were up there, too. Oh, how she complained about your father having the television on too loud. She thought he was hard of hearing. She said she was going to suggest to him that he get his ears checked out. Then she said your mother didn't know how to do windows. Apparently, there were smudges all over them." She chuckled and waved a hand in front of herself.

I stared at her. She smiled and chatted as if we were discussing the weather. I knew Hazel had complained about my parents, but I didn't want to hear the details. It was like eavesdropping, only I hadn't actually done the eavesdropping. Martha was forcing it on me.

"Is this all for you?" I asked, motioning toward her bag.

"That will do it. Of course, I'll be in next weekend to let the grandkids pick out their favorite candy. This is just for starters," she said and laughed.

I smiled back at her. Martha was middle-aged and wore too much makeup. She had always been a pleasant woman, but this wasn't a pleasant conversation. At least it wasn't pleasant for me.

"Great," I said and weighed the bag. "I hope they find the killer soon."

"Oh, I'm not worried. They did us all a favor," she said, digging through her purse. "I'm sure Hazel pushed someone too far, and it was curtains for her." She chuckled and pulled out a hairbrush, then put it back and kept digging.

"I don't mean to be rude, but that's not nice. She was a human being," I pointed out. I wanted to say so much more, but she was a customer and my mother had always taught me to be nice to customers. Or at least as nice as possible.

"Oh, Mia, I'm sorry. I guess I'm not being nice, am I? You're right. She was a human being and I'm sure there has to be someone somewhere that will grieve for her. I don't know who that could be, but I'm sure there's one somewhere." She chuckled again and held up her debit card while I rang up her candy.

I smiled and motioned toward the card reader. I didn't comment though. I wouldn't get anywhere with her. It did seem odd she was so jovial about Hazel being dead. Regardless of the fact that Hazel had made a nuisance of herself, it wasn't normal for someone to be happy about a murder.

I handed her a receipt. "Thank you, Martha."

"Thanks, sweetie," she said and took her candy and left.

"Who was that?" Mom asked, untying her apron with one hand. She had been making fudge in the back room and she carried out a tray of it to put in the display case.

"Martha Mayes. She seems inordinately pleased that Hazel was murdered."

"Really?" she asked, opening the display case.

The scent of fudge drifted over. As long as I had worked in the candy shop, I never tired of the smell of chocolate.

"Yes. Kind of strange, if you ask me."

"I heard she was under a lot of stress because Hazel called her to complain all the time. Vivian Jones said Martha had to see a therapist to help her cope."

"She seems to be coping just fine now," I said, sitting down on one of the stools behind the counter.

Mom chuckled. "I've interviewed three candidates for the part-time positions. Two more to go."

"That's great. We really need the help," I said. "I'd like to try out some new candy recipes and when we get the new employees trained, I'll be able to spend more time in the kitchen."

The bell over the door jingled as the door swung open.

It was Ethan. "Hi, Mrs. Jordan. Mia," he said, nodding.

I smiled. I was glad Ethan was worried about the town losing its Halloween theme. It made me feel a little kinder toward him.

"Hi," I said and tried not to smile too big.

"Hello, Ethan," Mom said. "Mia told me about the city council meeting. It would be a travesty if we lost the Halloween season. I'm glad you're going to help Mia come up with a website to help bring in more visitors."

Ethan smiled bigger. "I've talked to a number of people that are against canceling Halloween. I think if we all band together, we can stop it. Too much is at stake."

I nodded. "That's exactly what I was thinking," I said, slipping down off the stool and handing him the flyer I made the night before. "We can get together and have a think tank or something. Stir up some excitement over the season."

Ethan smiled as he read the flyer. "This a great idea. I bet we can come up with a solution to our problem."

"I think having a town council meeting for the business owners on Spooky Lane and Goblin Avenue is a fantastic idea," Mom said.

"And also for the citizens that are on our side. I think if we hand out these flyers, we could get a lot of people to show up," I said, leaning against the front counter.

"I knew I came to the right place," Ethan said. "This is exactly what we need. We can come up with a way to increase tourism. But I really think Jasper is right, and it's just a ploy by the mayor to get votes for another term."

"I don't doubt it," I said. "But we can't take any chances. We have to be proactive and get more business to the town."

"That's off the record, by the way," he said. "I don't want any trouble at work. The chief is the mayor's cousin."

I gasped. "I had no idea. I have been away too long. The chief of police is the mayor's cousin and the guy trying to stop the Halloween season is his brother-in-law. Now I've heard everything."

Ethan grinned. "Yup. Welcome to small town politics. You've still got to watch what you say to who around here."

I groaned. "That's one thing I didn't miss while I was gone."

"I've got more fudge to make," Mom said and excused herself.

"That fudge smells so good," he said. "I need to get some."

I nodded and went to the display case. "How much?"

"A quarter pound. I'll try not to eat it all at once," he said with a grin.

I used a spatula to scoop up a small slab my mother had already cut and put it into a paper bag. "Good luck with that. Ethan, do they know how Hazel died?"

"Complete autopsy results aren't back yet, but there was blunt force trauma to the back of her head."

"Oh, no," I said. "That's horrible." The thought that someone had hit her on the head made me cringe. Who did that to an elderly woman?

He nodded. "You just hate to hear about someone you know being murdered."

"Do you know Martha Mayes?" I asked him. I probably should have left well enough alone, but it bothered me that she was so happy about Hazel's murder.

He shrugged. "I know who she is, but I don't really know her. Why?"

I shrugged. "It just seems like a lot of people are happy Hazel is dead. It bugs me, I guess." I went to the cash register and rang up his fudge.

"It does seem like a lot of people are happy about it, but Hazel had a way with people, and it wasn't a good way," he said and ran his debit card through the card reader.

"I wonder if she knew she wasn't liked?" I mused.

He grinned. "I bet she did. I've talked to a lot of people about her death, and it seems she didn't care what other people thought of her."

I nodded. "I suppose so."

I hated to see anyone ganged up on and that's what this felt like. Someone needed to find her killer, and I thought I might just ask around a little. Maybe someone would tell me something they wouldn't tell the police. As awful as Hazel had been, she still deserved justice and we needed to get a killer off the streets.

Chapter Nine

"Good morning, Stella," I said, leaning up against her counter. "I'd like two crullers, please."

Stella sat on the stool behind the counter and sighed. "Really? You couldn't make it in here when those last customers were here?"

"What?" I asked, confused. "You mean the ones I just passed out on the sidewalk?"

"Yeah. Them."

"Um, why?" I asked.

"Because I just sat down and now I have to get up again." She narrowed her eyes at me.

"Oh. Sorry," I said. I didn't know how Stella stayed in business. She was almost as cranky as Hazel had been.

She sighed again and slid off the stool. "No problem." The sarcasm in her voice told me otherwise.

"Thanks," I said hesitantly as she washed her hands. I read the chalkboard on the wall while I waited for her to get my crullers. In the bottom left-hand corner, there was a note that said, *baker's dozen donuts, $9.00*. Beneath that, it said, *thirteen donuts*.

"So, if I get a baker's dozen donuts how many donuts will I get?" I asked, feeling a little wicked.

"A baker's dozen," Stella replied, putting plastic gloves on.

"What's the count?"

"Thirteen. Didn't your mother ever tell you how much a baker's dozen is?" She rolled her eyes.

"How come you wouldn't give Hazel thirteen donuts when she bought the baker's dozen?" I asked innocently.

"Because I didn't like her," she said and smiled. "Any other questions?"

I eyed her. Stella was something else. It made me wonder if she had something to do with Hazel's demise. "Stella, did you kill Hazel?"

I figured it wouldn't hurt to straight out ask. And maybe she'd give herself away in her response.

She snorted. "Please. Like I'd tell you. You'd run downtown and tell the police."

I gasped. "So, you did kill her?"

"Did I say that?" she asked, picking up two crullers and putting them into a white paper bag.

"No, but you didn't deny it either."

"Whatever. That's two dollars and fifty cents. I hope you have cash because I'm not running a credit card through for two-fifty."

I pulled two dollar bills and two quarters out of my pocket and handed them to her. "Stella, Labor Day is less than a week away. Maybe you should get some cute Halloween themed paper bags. Customers love them." I looked around the bakery. It was devoid of Halloween decorations.

"Why? The mayor is going to do away with the Halloween season. And good riddance to it, I say. I'm tired of this silliness."

"Why do you say that? You've lived here all your life. You have a bakery on Spooky Lane and you make your living off the Halloween season. I don't understand why you feel that way."

"Tell me something I don't know. This celebration has been a curse on the whole town. We need to change it up. People don't come to my bakery during the off-season because it's way over here near the edge of town and everyone thinks of this part of town as the Halloween part. They think we're only open during the holidays. They don't even think about coming here during the off-season."

"Why do you say that? We all get regular business during the off-season. And I see customers in here all the time."

"The Halloween theme makes us separate. And if we weren't separated over here, more people would come. I'm sure of it. You mark my words. When we get rid of Halloween, you'll see more business at your candy store."

"What do you mean separated? We aren't separated," I said. Stella wasn't making sense. People came to the candy store all year long and I couldn't imagine it was any different here at the donut shop.

"Sure we are. There are us, the Halloween freaks, and them. The regular business owners."

I looked at her, one eyebrow cocked. "That doesn't make sense," I said. "People go to whichever business they need or want. There's no separation."

Stella rolled her eyes. "It's like an imaginary divide in people's minds. Sure, some people shop here all year. But how many don't even come over here unless it's Halloween because they think we are seasonal businesses?"

She handed me the white paper bag. I had never thought of it like that and I suddenly wasn't sure she was completely wrong. On more than one occasion I had run into people that said they had forgotten about the candy store because they considered it a seasonal business. I had always assumed it was just a fluke and that other people didn't think that way. Was I wrong? Would business be better for all of us if we dropped the Halloween season?

"Hi Mia," Vince Moretti said, coming out of the back room with a tray of plain donuts. "It's a nice day out."

I glanced in his direction. "Hi, Vince." My mind was still turning over what Stella had said and I forgot to take a closer look at him to see if I could imagine him being younger and someone another woman would want to have an affair with.

"See?" Stella said. "I got you thinking, don't I?"

I shook my head. "No. No, you're wrong. I'm sure of it. Here's a flyer," I said, laying one on the counter. "We're going to work on saving the Halloween season and we would appreciate it if you would come out and support us. Thanks for the crullers."

"I hate the Halloween season. I won't be there," she said without looking at the flyer.

I headed out the door, letting it slam shut behind me. Stella had to be wrong. I would bet anything she was. Only, now there was this sinking feeling in the pit of my stomach that hadn't been there before. I took a deep breath and headed back to the candy store.

When I opened the door to the shop, there was a man in a black suit standing at the counter talking to my mother. He turned and smiled at me.

"Mia, dear, this is Detective Johnson. He wanted to ask us about finding Hazel." There was something in my mother's eyes that made me feel cautious.

"Oh," I said and went behind the counter to stand next to her.

He offered me his hand. "Pleased to meet you."

"Nice to meet you," I said, shaking his hand. I held the bag of crullers in my other hand, suddenly nervous.

"Can you tell me what happened the day you found Hazel Martin?" he asked me.

I glanced at my mother. "Sure. We had just gotten home from work and I looked over at Hazel's house. There was a scarecrow on the bench on her porch and I went to check it out. It was Hazel." My heart pounded in my chest and I hoped he couldn't hear it. I was being silly, I told myself. The detective was just doing his job and there was no reason to feel anxious. But, I did.

He jotted something down on a notepad. "When was the last time you spoke to Hazel before her death?"

"That morning. She didn't like that Stella Moretti down at the bakery wouldn't give her thirteen donuts."

"What?" he asked, looking up from the notepad, sounding confused.

"A baker's dozen. They disagreed on the number." I glanced at my mother again.

"I see," he said. "And why is that important?"

"It was important to Hazel. She insisted Stella give her thirteen donuts, but Stella only gave her twelve and it made her angry. Now that Hazel's dead, Stella's advertising that a baker's dozen is thirteen." I didn't think it would mean anything to him, but I wanted him to know. I also wanted to tell him about the affair Hazel had had with Vince Moretti, but I wasn't sure my mother would like it if I told him.

"I see," he repeated and made a note.

"We already told the police what happened," I pointed out.

I didn't know Pumpkin Hollow had a detective. I thought I would ask Ethan about it. If the city had money to pay for a detective when we rarely had murders or violent crime, then why did the mayor say we didn't have money for the Halloween season?

"I understand. I just want to go over everything," he said without looking up from his notepad. "Can you tell me anything else about your relationship with Hazel Martin?"

I shook my head when he looked up at me. "There's nothing to tell. She was our neighbor for all my life. Sometimes she would come in and buy candy." I shrugged. If he had spoken to many people, he already knew she was difficult to get along with. I was beginning to wish I had never checked on Hazel. No one would be questioning me if I hadn't gone to see about the scarecrow sitting on her bench.

The detective asked a series of questions we had already answered with the police and then bought some fudge before leaving. When the door closed behind him, I looked at Mom.

"I don't like this."

She gave me a small smile. "I'm sure it's fine. The police want to make sure they get the whole story. Investigating a murder can't be easy."

I opened the paper bag and took a cruller out and handed the bag to her.

"I don't like being asked the same questions over and over. I feel like they have their eye on us," I said and took a bite of my cruller.

"I don't think that's it. I'm sure they just want to put the killer behind bars."

"You're probably right," I said carefully. "I think it had to be someone that knew Hazel really well. The problem is, no one liked her and it could be anyone."

"I bet someone liked her. I don't know who it would be, of course," Mom said and took a bite of her cruller. "These are always so fresh."

"Did you like her, mom?" My mother was a look-on-the-bright-side kind of person. I admired that in her, but I had a more suspicious nature. People usually had a reason for doing the things they did and sometimes it wasn't for a good reason.

Mom studied her cruller before answering. "I have to admit, she was difficult. We all knew that. But I can't say I disliked her, either. She just had her issues."

I sighed. "Issues, indeed."

I took another bite of my cruller. Stella Moretti was the person I thought the police should look at closely. She had more reason than anyone to kill Hazel. If I could just find more evidence, she could be arrested, and Pumpkin Hollow would get back to normal.

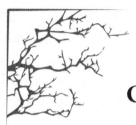

Chapter Ten

By the time I pulled into my driveway, I was worn out from worrying about the detective stopping by the shop as well as whether the Halloween season was hurting our business. I was torn. I had all these wonderful childhood memories of all the Halloween events through the years. I could pull out any photo album in my parents' house and flip through countless pictures of my younger sister and me dressed as princesses, witches, and mermaids, enjoying the season as it was meant to be. Would we lose all that? *Should* we lose all that? The taxes for the business district where the candy shop was located were high. They had to be. They supported many of the Halloween activities. But other businesses in the community supported the Halloween season, too. I sighed. I needed a hot shower and a good night's sleep.

I got out of my car and looked over at Hazel's house. No one had stopped by yet to check that everything was in order. I knew she had to have relatives. Where were they? I hoped at least one person in her life grieved for her. It would mean they had loved her. As my eyes traveled over the white bench on the porch, a picture of Hazel's slumped-over body flashed across my mind. I shook my head to clear it. I didn't want to see anything like that ever again.

I turned to head to my house when I heard someone swear. I turned back toward Hazel's house. Mr. Gott lived in the house on the other side and he was working on a lawnmower, pulling on the starter over and over. He pulled it and released it. Pulled it and released it. He straightened up a moment and looked at the mower, hands on his hips.

Mr. Gott was elderly, and I expected it took a lot out of him to get the lawn mower started. I headed over to see if I could help out.

"Hi, Mr. Gott," I said as I approached.

He turned and looked at me, his white hair falling across his forehead. He pushed it back and smiled at me. His grass had grown far past the legal length the homeowners association allowed and I was sure he was worried he would get a letter.

"Hello, Mia, how are you?" he asked brightly.

"I'm fine. Having trouble with the lawnmower?"

He nodded. "The stupid thing doesn't want to work. Not that I blame it. I don't like working, either," he said with a chuckle. Mr. Gott was usually good humored, except for when he had a run-in with Hazel. It seemed his long, overgrown grass had been an issue for her on more than one occasion. An issue that she had never allowed to slide past her.

"Can I try?" I asked.

He nodded and motioned for me to go ahead.

I set my purse down on the sidewalk, then went to the mower, took hold of the starter handle and pulled. The engine sputtered, then went silent. I tried again, pulling and releasing quickly like my father had taught me years ago. It sputtered and stopped several times, then caught.

I looked up at Mr. Gott and he was smiling. "Thank you, Mia!" he said over the roar of the engine.

"I'll do it for you," I said, taking hold of the handle. The day had turned out warm and Mr. Gott was already sweating. His front yard was nice and flat and not very large. I was tired, but I figured I could do it in less than fifteen minutes.

He nodded and shouted, "thank you!"

I picked up my purse and set it on his porch, then got to work pushing the mower around the yard. The mower rolled easily and the physical exercise felt surprisingly good. I was careful to push the mower in straight lines to give it a neat appearance.

When I finished, Mr. Gott handed me a glass of ice water. "You don't know how much I appreciate this. I think this lawn will be the death of me one day."

"It's no problem," I said between gulps of water. The water felt good and tasted clean, washing down my parched throat.

"I need to get an electric mower. I'm tired of fighting with this one," he commented.

I nodded. "The gas ones are hard to start," I said, looking at him. "Mr. Gott, did the police question you about Hazel's death?"

He snorted. "Of course they did. Like I would know anything. I told them I wasn't a bit sorry she was dead though. I doubt anyone is."

"You told them that? Aren't you afraid to tell the police something like that?" I asked.

"What for? It's the truth and I find you should always tell the police the truth. She was always reporting me for any little thing, plus she let her cat out to do its business beneath my rose bushes." Mr. Gott's lips pressed together in a straight line.

"Oh," I said. I didn't tell him Hazel didn't have a cat and it must have been someone else's. "Well, I feel kind of bad she died the way she did. And the killer dressing her as a scarecrow just added insult to injury."

"She had it coming. I'd say someone was trying to send a message. That woman should have kept her mouth shut and her nose out of people's business. I don't blame whoever killed her, not one bit. Someone should have done it sooner."

I was taken aback by his anger. I nodded. "She was a busybody, but I don't think she deserved to be killed."

"I won't miss her a bit. I couldn't stand the woman." He shook his head. "Nope. I won't miss her."

I was shocked. I had underestimated the anger people felt toward Hazel.

"Did you happen to see or hear anything unusual that day?"

"Not a thing," he said, shaking his head again. He had white bushy eyebrows that came together when he was angry. "It's not like anyone in this town will miss her. She was a blight on Pumpkin Hollow's behind."

I studied Mr. Gott a moment. Something about his reaction bothered me more than other people's reactions had. Since I had returned home, he had seemed a little off. He got angry easily and didn't seem himself. Maybe spending so much time alone was the reason.

"Well, I had better get going," I said, handing him the glass back. "I'll see you later, Mr. Gott."

"Okay," he said, smiling. "Thanks again for mowing my lawn. I wish all neighbors were as kind as you. Tell your mother I said hello."

"You're welcome, and I'll tell her," I said over my shoulder and retrieved my purse.

As I stepped over onto Hazel's property, a police cruiser pulled up to the curb of Mr. Gott's house. I stopped and squinted my eyes at the car. Ethan waved from behind the steering wheel. I waited for him to get out of the car.

"Hi Mia, how are you?" he called.

I nodded. "I'm fine," I said and headed back toward Mr. Gott's house. "What are you doing in this neck of the woods?"

"I just need to speak to Mr. Gott. How are you, Mr. Gott?" he asked him.

"I'm fine. What do you want?" he asked, sounding curt.

"I just need to go over what we discussed the other day," Ethan said.

"Well, it hasn't changed any. Did you expect it to?"

Ethan smiled. "I did not expect it to change, no sir. But you know how we police are. We like to get all the facts and then make sure they're accurate."

Mr. Gott snorted. "You all waste your time and the taxpayers' money."

I smiled at Ethan. "I better get home and help my mother with dinner. I'll talk to you later."

"I'll see you later," Ethan said.

"Good bye, Mr. Gott," I called over my shoulder.

It seemed odd that Ethan was questioning Mr. Gott again, and I wondered if the detective had also stopped by to talk to him. I wished I had asked Mr. Gott that question. Mr. Gott was a nice neighbor, but sometimes he could be a little cantankerous. If Ethan wasn't careful, he would get an earful.

It was a little crazy that Mr. Gott would admit to being glad Hazel was dead to the police, and I wondered if that was why the police kept stopping by to question him. He would be better off keeping his opinion to himself, at least when the police were involved.

I sighed and opened my front door. The invigorating feeling I had gotten from mowing had worn off and I was tired again.

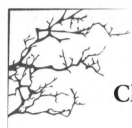

Chapter Eleven

"WE'RE GETTING A SHIPMENT of supplies tomorrow," Mom said as she stood at the stove, stirring a bubbling pot of spaghetti sauce.

"Halloween supplies?" I asked, mixing some minced garlic into softened butter for the garlic bread. Spaghetti night was one of my favorites.

"Yes, along with the sugar and regular supplies. I hope they don't take the Halloween season away from us. It would be a shame."

"I don't think they will. Or at least, I hope not. But if they do, candy still sells. The business will be fine." I knew we would be okay. I just didn't want to lose our heritage of Halloween-themed candy making.

"I hate that all this is going on so close to the start of the season," she said. "Seems like they could at least wait until after it's over to decide on it."

"It will be fine, Ann," my dad said. He was leaning on the kitchen doorframe, watching us cook. "Things have a way of working out. If we lose the Halloween season, there are all the other holidays to make candy for."

"I know, I know," she said with a frown. "It just seems a shame. The Halloween season is what makes Pumpkin Hollow special. Oh, and I've decided on the two part-time employees. Andrea Stone and Lisa Anderson."

"I think those are great choices. And I think it will really help us out," I said. I knew and liked both girls and it made me happy Mom had chosen them.

The doorbell rang, and we all looked toward the front door.

"I'll get it," Dad said and went into the living room.

I cut the loaves of French bread in half and spread the garlic butter on them. I made it nice and thick so it would soak down into the bread as it baked. Garlic was a favorite ingredient of mine. It came right behind chocolate.

"There's someone here to see the two of you," Dad said, when he came back into the kitchen.

I looked up and Ethan stood in the doorway.

"Hey," he said, smiling at my mom and then me. "Sorry to intrude. But I needed to ask you both some questions."

I narrowed my eyes at him. Hadn't we already been over what we had seen and done the night Hazel's body was discovered?

"Oh, sure, Ethan," Mom said hesitantly. "Would you like to stay for dinner? We're having spaghetti and meatballs."

I looked at my mother and gave her a warning look. I did not want to spend dinner being quizzed about Hazel's death. Besides that, my sister Christy and her husband John were coming for dinner.

"Oh, no thank you," Ethan said, sticking his hands into his pockets. "I still have to finish up my shift."

"Mia, get Ethan a bottle of water. He's probably thirsty," Mom said.

I sighed under my breath and stood up, wiping my hands on a dishtowel. I got a bottle of water from the fridge and handed it to Ethan.

"Thank you, Mia. Now, can you tell me, did any of you see anything suspicious at Mrs. Martin's house in the days leading up to the murder?"

"I never noticed anything," my dad said.

"Me either," I said. "Everything seemed normal."

"Hazel was tending her flower beds in her front yard a lot those last few days. She did that when she wanted to keep an especially close eye on someone in the neighborhood," Mom said. "Maybe there was someone suspicious hanging around?"

Ethan nodded, pulled a small notebook out of his pocket, and made a note. "But nothing you saw for yourself?"

"No, not really. Hazel made the rounds of the neighborhood quite often. Perhaps one of the other neighbors saw something unusual, or maybe she talked to them about something," Mom said.

"We've already been over this," I pointed out. "We really didn't see anything."

"Mr. Gott said there was a loud noise the morning she died. He thought it was coming from Mrs. Martin's house on the side closest to your house. Did any of you hear anything?"

I shook my head and turned on the oven to preheat.

Wait a minute. Mr. Gott said he didn't hear anything that day. I turned to look at him.

"I didn't hear a thing," Mom said.

"Are you sure he said he heard a noise? Because a few minutes ago he told me he didn't hear or see anything unusual that day," I said.

"Hm," Ethan said. "Maybe he's confused which day it was that he heard the sound."

"Maybe," I said. Mr. Gott was getting up there in age. He could have been confused about the whole thing.

"And you said you saw her at the candy store the morning of the murder?" he asked, looking at me.

I nodded. "Yes, that's what I told you the last time we talked. Hazel stopped in and was upset that she couldn't get a baker's dozen of donuts. Which, by the way, is what Stella Moretti is now selling. Thirteen donuts, not twelve. I think it's odd that as soon as Hazel died, she started selling them that way to other customers, but she refused to sell them that way to Hazel."

"Stella never liked Hazel," Dad said. "Whenever I went into the bakery, she complained about Hazel. But I think she just liked to complain about other people, to tell you the truth."

"I see," Ethan said and made a note in his notebook.

"I didn't know Pumpkin Hollow had a detective," I said, thinking about Detective Johnson. "The mayor is complaining about not having money for the Halloween season, yet we can afford a detective?"

"Oh, that's just Johnson. We're borrowing him from Greenwood. We don't have one on staff. That's why I'm interviewing people, too," he said, holding up his notebook.

"Still, it's got to cost something," I said.

"That's true," he said. "But I'm not privy to that kind of information."

The front door opened, and we all turned to look. My sister Christy and her husband, John, walked through the door. Christy held a bowl of salad in her hands.

"Hey, everyone," she said and looked at Ethan. "Hi, Ethan."

"Hi Christy, hi John. How are you two?"

"We're fine," Christy said. "Are you joining us for dinner?"

He shook his head. "No, I'm just asking your mom and sister a few questions about Hazel Martin's death."

"That was terrible. But I can kind of see where she got on people's nerves." She set the bowl of salad on the table. "Hazel wasn't anyone's favorite person."

"You don't know anything about her death, do you?" I asked her. I was being a smart aleck.

She smirked. "Yeah, right after I had my nails done, I stopped by and stuffed her with straw. You have to admit it was kind of fitting, in a way."

"What do you mean?" Ethan asked.

She shrugged. "She hated anything to do with the Halloween season, and she hated people decorating their yards. In death, she was turned into a great big Halloween decoration for her own yard. The killer's got a wicked sense of humor, pardon the pun."

John chuckled. "That is kind of twisted."

"Don't make fun of the dead," Mom said. "It's not right."

"She isn't going to come back and haunt me. At least, I don't think she will," Christy said and sat down at the table.

"She would if she could," I said and put the garlic bread into the oven.

"Well, I suppose I should let you folks enjoy your dinner," Ethan said, closing his notebook. I think he had had enough of our less than sensitive humor.

"You should stay. We'll be nice," Christy told him. "Or, we'll try, anyway."

"I've got a shift to finish," Ethan said. "You all will let me know if you remember anything, right?"

I nodded. "You'll be the first person we call. I hope you find the killer. I'd hate for them to be running around town, maybe thinking about who to murder next."

"Oh, Mia," Mom said. "Don't say that. I'm sure whoever it is won't kill anyone else. At least I hope not."

"I'll see you to the door," my dad said and led the way for Ethan.

"So, are you two suspects?" John asked when Ethan had left the kitchen.

I rolled my eyes. "We better not be. I was trying to do a good deed when I went over there that night. I was just checking on things and really regret it now."

"Never regret a good deed, dear," Mom said. "It will come back to you some day."

I sighed and sat down. All I wanted was for Hazel's killer to be arrested and the Halloween season saved.

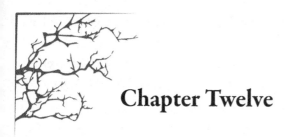

Chapter Twelve

I t was Friday evening, and I was standing on the gazebo at Pumpkin Hollow Park waiting for other Halloween business owners to show up. I had handed out flyers to everyone I could think of and posted them all over town. The Baptist church loaned me some folding chairs, and I set them up in rows, hoping they would all be filled for the meeting. I was pleased we already had a small group eagerly waiting for the meeting to begin and my fingers were crossed, hoping for more. I had brought taffy, fudge, and candy corn, and put them on a table along with iced tea and chips. I hoped the snacks would put people in a good mood and help facilitate new ideas to save the Halloween season.

A police cruiser pulled up and parked at the curb. I squinted my eyes and saw it was Ethan. I wasn't sure whether to be happy he was here, or stay mad at him because he was asking my mother and me about the murder again.

He got out of his car and sauntered over. "Hey, Mia," he said with a nod.

"Hi Ethan," I returned. I had a paper with notes I wanted to remember, folded and creased in my hands, and I looked down at it now and straightened it out.

Ethan looked around. "It looks like we are going to have a nice turnout."

I smiled. *We*. I wasn't sure we were a 'we', but whatever.

"I was hoping for a few more people," I said. I glanced at my watch. We still had five minutes until we started. Fourteen business owners had shown up along with a handful of others, and if this was all that was going to show up, then I was less than excited with that number. Now was the time to stand up for our rights and the more that showed up, the better chance we had at success.

"Give it a few more minutes," he said, leaning against the gazebo wall.

"Anything new on the murder?" I asked while we waited.

He shook his head. "If there is, I haven't been informed."

"Seems like you could spend your time better by looking for more clues and not talking to the same people over and over."

If I could, I would have sucked those words right back into my mouth. I was thinking them, but I hadn't meant to say them.

He gave me a sideways look. "I'm just doing my job. I'm not pointing fingers at anyone."

"Sorry," I said and looked away.

"Mia, I know you didn't kill Hazel. Do you think I suspect you?"

I shrugged. "It seems like you might have your eye on me or my mother."

He chuckled. "Guilty conscience? Maybe I should take a closer look."

I gasped. "No, I do not have a guilty conscience! I just don't like being accused of murder after I did a good deed by checking on Hazel. Or rather, by checking on the odd Halloween decoration on her porch which turned out to be her."

"You were never accused," he said. "I think your imagination may be getting the best of you. Don't worry about it."

"Fine, I won't," I said as three more cars pulled up and parked at the curb. I smiled when Amanda and Brian got out of one of the cars.

"We just might have a lot of support," Ethan said, watching as two more cars pulled up behind the other three.

"We might," I said. "Ethan, can I ask you why you want this?"

"It's my town, too. I protect and serve it every day and I grew up here, just like you did. Why wouldn't I want to save the Halloween season?"

I nodded and thought I might be a bit of a jerk in the way I was treating him. "I'm glad you're here to support us," I said.

He studied me a minute. "My parents wanted me to be a lawyer or a doctor. But I couldn't imagine moving away. I guess I could have come back after getting my education, but I had no desire to be either one of those professions. I like what I do."

"Yeah? It takes a lot of guts to go against what your parents want," I said, nodding.

"Why did you come back?" he asked.

I smiled and looked away. "I had big dreams. A part of me couldn't wait to get away from this small town where everyone seems to know everything about everyone. But when I got out there in the great big world, I didn't know what to do with myself. I got a few degrees, decided I wasn't happy, and moved home."

"Some people just take longer to learn," he said with a grin. "At least I was smart enough to stay where I belonged."

"Some of us take a little longer to figure things out," I said, trying not to sound defensive.

I glanced at my watch again. It was 7:00. "Well, here goes," I said. I stood up and went to the edge of the gazebo.

"Excuse me," I said as loudly as I could. No one turned in my direction. A microphone would have made it easier, but I didn't know anyone that had one. I looked at Ethan.

He straightened up and cupped his hands around his mouth. "Ladies and gentleman. Can we have your attention?"

When people turned in our direction and stopped talking, Ethan continued. "Mia Jordan would like your full attention, please."

I smiled at him and then turned to the small crowd. "As most of you know, the city council is considering ending the Halloween season. I know most of you grew up here in this town and have fond memories of Halloween celebrations and traditions. It would be a shame to lose them. It's what makes our town unique. I believe we need to fight for the town and for the season. We need to get together and figure out a way to make extra money, both for ourselves and to make the season profitable for the city. I called this meeting so we could put our heads together and come up with some ideas. Does anyone have any suggestions?"

Fagan stood up.

"I say we get rid of the mayor and his no-good brother-in-law. The two of them are trying to run this town into the ground. I don't know how he got into office to begin with."

I glanced at Ethan. "This meeting isn't about getting rid of the mayor. It's about figuring out what to do to save the Halloween season."

Fagan rolled his eyes and sighed. "Getting rid of the mayor will save the season."

"Yes, but, I think voting the mayor out of office will take a long time. We need something short term and more specific to saving the Halloween season."

"Who said anything about voting the mayor out?" Fagan said and grinned, looking around at those closest to him. There was a murmur that went up and some heads nodded in agreement.

"Why don't we concentrate on strategies to improve business?" Ethan said. "I think that would be more productive."

I gave Ethan a look that said, "thanks for being here."

"Fine," Fagan said. "You mentioned advertising and using the Internet to bring in more business at the city council meeting. Have you done anything with that yet?"

"I've been working on a city website focusing on the Halloween season with a visitor's guide, but I'm not done with it," I said. "It shouldn't be too much longer though."

"I think that's our best bet," he said, nodding. "People need to know what we have to offer. In recent years it seems like we've slipped off of many people's radars."

I nodded. "I think so too. We need to revamp our image and let people know we're here."

"We could always advertise that we had a murder here. People would be nosy enough to come and check us out," Fagan said and laughed.

I sighed and rolled my eyes. "We need to stick to the topic." I glanced at Ethan. Fagan was another person that didn't seem to mind that Hazel was dead.

Carl Givens from the gift shop stood up. "I was thinking maybe we could have town guides to take visitors around to various events on the weekends. We have the horse-drawn wagons for hayrides at the haunted farmhouse. What if we extended it and had a fixed route to take people from place to place? Residents could be told in advance so they would be careful of the horses, and people could pay to ride."

"That's not a bad idea," I said. "I like that." I looked at Ethan and he smiled and nodded.

"I was thinking we might add a county fair of some sort," Erica Johnson said, standing up. "You know, like an old fashioned one. We could charge for events. It would only have to be on weekends during the Halloween season and it would provide part-time jobs to townsfolk."

I smiled and nodded. People had been thinking about saving the Halloween season. They cared what happened, and I felt my eyes tear up. I had been afraid no one would care, and I had never been so happy to be wrong.

Elle Simpkins stood up, flipping her red hair over her shoulder. "We need someone to judge the pumpkin carving contest this weekend. Will you do it, Mia? You could be our key contact person for all things Halloween. We've never been organized enough to have a contact person."

"We used to have someone," Fagan pointed out. "It was the mayor. But ever since Stan Goodall was voted in, he's refused to do it. That's the real reason the Halloween season has suffered. Our mayor doesn't care about our town."

There was a murmur that went up, punctuated with several "Yeah" and "that's right" comments.

I didn't want this to turn into a political argument, so I spoke up. "I've never done anything like that before, but I can try. At least, temporarily, until we can find someone permanent."

I was getting excited as people talked about ideas. We might really be able to save the Halloween season. I glanced around as people tossed ideas around and I noticed Stella wasn't there, along with a couple other business owners. I decided not to worry about it. We had far more business owners show up than were missing and most importantly, we had some excitement going on. People really wanted to save the town.

I looked at Ethan. "This might work. I'm excited."

He nodded. "Me too. I think we've got something here."

I sat down on the step and listened in on the conversations. With some organization, we could become a force to be reckoned with.

Chapter Thirteen

I was sitting on the gazebo steps with a brown bag lunch the next day, feeling smug. I had left the meeting the night before walking on air. The turnout had been delightful and as far as I was concerned, we would not lose the Halloween season. I felt it deep in my bones. We would fight city hall if need be, but we would not lose the celebration we all held so dear. I took a bite of my tuna sandwich and checked my phone for messages. I sighed. No one from my old life had checked up on me since I had moved home and I was feeling a little dejected in spite of the successful meeting we'd just had.

"I'll just have to renew acquaintances here in Pumpkin Hollow," I murmured.

"Well, Mia Jordan. I heard all about your meeting," I heard a voice say.

I looked up from my phone. Stella Moretti stood in front of me, her hands on her hips.

"Excuse me?" I asked.

"That stupid Halloween season. It's a nuisance. One this town can't afford. I don't care how many people tell you they'll help you save the celebrations, they won't follow through. Oh, they'll tell you they will, but they won't. I know these people."

She wagged a finger at me and her too-long bangs blew up in the light breeze.

"Stella, what do you mean? We had a good turnout last night. I think we can do this," I said, looking up at her. "I was a little disappointed that you didn't come."

She snorted. "Why do you even care? You moved away for what, ten years? Twelve? Why did you bother to come back? A young educated woman like you could do anything with your life."

"Yes, I can. And what I want to do now that I'm home, is renew the town's values and traditions that I grew up with. Why are you against that, Stella? Your bakery is one of the Halloween businesses. It seems like you'd want to be more successful." I was confused by her hostility. We all stood to make more money with increased business, and if we could build a solid plan, we would have that increased business.

"Are you kidding me? Those stupid celebrations! I would make far more money if I could run my business like a normal bakery, like I told you before. But no, since it's located where it is, I have to continue the Halloween theme. Why, I could branch out and make wedding cakes! But no one will come to a Halloween bakery for a wedding cake. Why don't you get it?" Her lips pressed tightly together and I could see where her bright red lipstick bled into the fine lines around her mouth.

I shook my head. "Why not? Why not bake wedding cakes and advertise them? Put pictures in the advertisement so people can see you offer more than just Halloween themed baked goods. I think it would be good if we all did that. It would help draw new customers in."

She snorted and looked up to the sky, then back at me. "You are one clueless woman, aren't you? This town is too small. No one thinks outside the box. We're stuck with this Halloween theme unless we completely do away with it."

"We are not going to do away with it. I can assure you of that," I said, looking her dead in the eye. "And I would be glad to help you bring more business into the bakery in any way I can. Honestly, Stella, we're all in this together."

She sighed and looked at me. When she didn't say anything else, I looked down at the sandwich I still held in my hand.

"I guess that answers the question of why you moved back, doesn't it?"

I looked up at her, puzzled. "What do you mean?"

"You ride in here like the Lone Ranger to save the day. But all you really want is to make money off all us hard-working business owners. I bet you'll be offering all kinds of business services—for a big fat fee."

I gasped. "Stella Moretti, that never even crossed my mind. My parents own a candy store. Why wouldn't I want to help them and the other business owners do more business? My moving back had nothing to do with trying to make money off of people."

"Yeah, we'll see about that. I've got to go. My husband is minding the shop. But I can tell you I'm not the only one that feels this way. I can have a little meeting, too, you know. I can gather together the people that want to drop Halloween altogether." With that, she turned and strode back to her car.

I sighed and looked at my sandwich again. It made no sense to me that people wouldn't support our efforts to save

Halloween. I suddenly felt queasy and wrapped up the rest of my sandwich and put it back in the bag.

A police cruiser pulled up to the curb and when Ethan got out, I felt myself smile. *Stop that*, I scolded myself.

"Hey," he said when he got to me.

"Hey yourself," I said. "I just had an unpleasant conversation with Stella Moretti."

"Oh?" he asked and sat next to me on the step.

I nodded, looking at my feet. This whole thing was now making me feel a little depressed. I looked back up at him. "She doesn't want to save Halloween. I don't get it. It's our heritage. It's what we're known for."

"Don't let the naysayers worry you. There will be people who won't support us. But what difference does it make? We'll just keep working on it."

"She said she was going to have a meeting with others that want the Halloween season to end. The mayor is on their side, so do we even have a chance?" I tried to keep the whine out of my voice, but I wasn't sure I was successful.

"I still think the mayor isn't serious. And we have a lot of people on our side, too. It's way too early to give up."

"I'm not giving up," I protested. I hated sounding like a whiner, but if I had to be honest, I guess I was. "I will fight for this. I don't want to do anything less."

"Good. I'm glad to hear it. I think it's providential that you came home when you did. We need you. Your education will come in handy to help save the season."

I smiled at him. I couldn't help myself. Lies about spiders in my hair or not, he didn't seem so bad these days. Perhaps he had grown up since seventh grade.

"I hope it is providential. We'll put everything into it and we'll make this happen," I said. I didn't want to tell him what Stella had said about my moving home to make money off the business owners. It hurt my feelings and had never even entered my mind.

"I have a good feeling about all of this," he said.

"Have you heard anything new about Hazel's murder?" I asked. I probably sounded nosy, but I had to ask. There was a murderer on the streets of Pumpkin Hollow, and we needed that person put in jail.

"Not much. They're still interviewing people. Mia, you do believe me when I say I don't suspect you, right?"

I took in a deep breath. "Yes, I know. I know you're just doing your job and I'm not taking it personally." That wasn't the complete truth, but I wasn't going to let on. I just wanted the killer off the street and as long as Ethan didn't suspect me, then I was fine.

"Good. Well, I've got to get back to work. And don't worry about the Halloween season. We're going on with it as planned."

I hoped he was right. In the meantime I would brainstorm some ideas to get things going. I intended to make this Halloween season the best we had ever had. I wasn't sure how I was going to go about it, but I would manage it somehow.

Chapter Fourteen

"HI MIA," AMANDA SAID when I walked through the door of the coffee shop. "I was wondering where you'd gotten to. What are you doing?"

"Trying to wake up. I stayed up too late last night and I need some caffeine," I said, looking up at the menu board. The mummy's curse latte sounded good. It had vanilla and almond flavors.

"I'm impressed with the turnout for last night's meeting," she said. "Everyone had good ideas."

"I was impressed, too," I said, brightening. "I really think we can turn this town around. And I think I'll have the mummy's curse. With a shot of espresso, please."

"With whip?" she asked.

I nodded. "There's no curse unless there's some whip on it. Presuming the curse part is all the calories in it." I had given up on trying to cut back on calories by leaving the whipped cream off my drinks. For today, at least.

She chuckled. "That's true. I happen to love this kind of curse though."

I looked around the shop. At one table sat a young mother with her toddler in tow and at another sat Mr. Gott. He was reading a newspaper and had a cup of coffee sitting on the table.

I turned back to Amanda. "Amanda, how has business been for you guys?" I asked in a lowered voice.

She shrugged. "Not too bad. People will always buy coffee. It'll pick up any day though, just like everyone else's business will pick up, but it could always be better outside of the Halloween season."

I nodded. "We could use a boost in business, too. I'll have that city website done soon, but I'm not ready to unveil it yet."

"That's great. Maybe Brian can hire you to build one for us? He's been talking about putting one up, but you know him. He's a procrastinator."

I smiled and pushed Stella's accusation that I had come home to make money off the merchants out of my mind. I would help in any way I could.

"Websites aren't hard to build, but it does take a little time."

Amanda was right about Brian. He really was a procrastinator. He had promised to take me to the winter formal in the tenth grade and hadn't gotten around to ordering a tux for himself until the day before the dance. It was too late by then and he had worn a too-large suit of his father's. I had been embarrassed, and a little irritated when he hadn't gotten the tux after more than a month of almost daily reminders from me.

She handed me my latte, and I inhaled the sweet vanilla scent. "That smells so good. Thanks," I said, and looked at Mr. Gott sitting at a table by himself. I dug through my purse for my debit card to pay for the drink.

"Don't worry about it, Mia. This one is on the house," Amanda said.

"Are you sure? I can pay."

"Positive," she said, smiling. "You organizing the meeting last night deserves a free coffee. Don't worry about it."

"Well, be sure and stop by the shop for some fudge. Mom's been working on some new Halloween flavors. We'll make a trade for the coffee."

"Sounds like a plan. I love your mother's fudge," she said.

I picked up my cup of coffee and headed over to Mr. Gott's table. He didn't look up as I stood by his table, so I cleared my throat. He still didn't look up. I glanced at Amanda and shrugged.

"Good morning, Mr. Gott," I said loud and clear. I looked at his cup of coffee. There was no lid on the cup and his coffee was black. Nothing fancy for Mr. Gott.

He looked up from his paper and focused his eyes on me.

"Morning? It's nearly noon. But I guess by a technicality it's still morning," he said.

"That it is," I said. "May I have a seat?"

He nodded and motioned to the one across from him.

"Thank you. How are you doing, Mr. Gott?"

"I'm fine. I don't have a pesky neighbor to bother me anymore, so I guess you could say I'm doing all right," he said and grinned.

I smiled at him. I didn't know what to say to that. I still thought it was a shame so many people weren't the least bit sad Hazel had died, but at the same time, she had brought so much dislike on herself.

"So, Mr. Gott, did you happen to hear anything the day Hazel died?" I asked. I wondered what he would say after telling me he hadn't heard anything and then telling Ethan he had heard a loud noise.

He grinned bigger. "I noticed the neighborhood is quieter."

I sighed and shook my head. "We all noticed that. I just wondered if there was anything the police might have missed is all."

He shrugged. "I don't know. I do recall hearing you scream and the police and ambulance came with sirens blaring. Is that enough?"

"But what about before all that happened on the day Hazel died? Or the night before? Did you hear anything then?"

"I can't remember," he said, and turned the page of his newspaper.

I sighed and watched him read his newspaper. This had been a pointless exchange. For something else to say, I asked, "The Halloween season is almost here. That's exciting, isn't it?"

He scowled. "I don't know how you can call it exciting. Those pesky tourists stop in and they dilly-dally, driving slowly up and down the streets causing traffic jams. They should have done away with that Halloween season years ago." He folded his newspaper over, rattling the pages.

"Now, Mr. Gott, the town relies on the Halloween season for revenue. And so many people just really enjoy it."

"I don't know why you'd think people enjoy it. It's a mess. And who wants to look at goblins, mummies, and vampires for months on end?" He snorted and looked at his paper again.

I sighed. Trying to get him to change his mind was pointless.

"Well, Mr. Gott, it's fun for the kids. And if you are so against it, why are you drinking coffee in a Halloween coffee shop when there are other regular coffee shops in town?"

"If you must know, it's closer to my house," he said and stood up. "I've got business to attend to now. You have yourself a wonderful day and don't let any witches cast a spell on you." With a wink, he picked up his cup of coffee and left the shop.

I sighed again. We needed to change the minds of some of the townsfolk, along with bringing in new business. We had a big job ahead of us.

Amanda plopped down in the chair Mr. Gott had vacated. "No love lost between Mr. Gott and Hazel, huh?"

I shook my head and took a sip of my latte. "Not a bit. But then, there was no love lost between Hazel and anyone else, either. It's odd that no one saw or heard anything, don't you think? I mean, whoever stuffed her clothes with straw and sat her on that bench did it in broad daylight. Why didn't anyone see it?"

She shook her head. "I really don't know. Has Ethan mentioned if the police have figured anything out yet?" she asked.

"No, nothing new. At least, he hasn't told me if he knows anything. But if I had to put my money on someone, I would vote Stella Moretti. She really couldn't stand Hazel and she's so against the Halloween season. She's just a cantankerous person. Cantankerous. I've always wanted to use that word in a sentence," I said and giggled.

"You're so learned," she said and laughed.

"It's all that education. At least it isn't going to waste."

"I wonder what Stella would say if you flat-out asked her if she murdered Hazel," she asked.

"I asked her that the other day."

Amanda gasped. "What did she say when you asked?"

"She was flippant, as usual. To be honest, she didn't really answer my question."

And that was what made me doubly suspicious when it came to Stella Moretti. The woman wasn't right in more ways than one and if she had killed Hazel, I was going to find out.

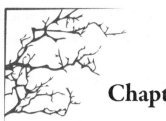

Chapter Fifteen

AMANDA AND I DECIDED to ask Stella if she had killed Hazel. Maybe we were crazy. But maybe she would be in a talking mood and we would find out something important. I had already asked once, but she hadn't been forthcoming. Two of us asking might change things. The killer needed to be caught before the tourists caught wind of what had happened. On the other hand, maybe a rumor that a murderer was on the loose would help business. Pumpkin Hollow had a reputation for being family friendly and a killer on the loose was the exact opposite of that. But maybe we could draw in another type of crowd with the rumor; those that liked slash and gore. I shivered. That wasn't exactly my kind of Halloween.

I pushed open the door to Sweet Goblin Bakery and Amanda followed me inside. I was dressed as Dorothy from the Wizard of Oz and Amanda was Tinker Bell. We both loved dressing up on the weekends during the Halloween season.

Stella was sitting on her stool behind the counter, reading her newspaper. It was Saturday, the first day of the Labor Day weekend, and I expected the crowds to be here any moment, but the bakery was empty except for the three of us. I wished Stella would have worn a costume, but that was never going to happen.

"Good morning, Stella," I said. The bakery display case was filled with all sorts of Halloween themed donuts. Vampire's blush raspberry-filled donuts, mummy cupcakes, and black cat cookies. It surprised me a little. What wouldn't have surprised me was if Stella had said "forget it" and not done anything Halloween themed at all.

She glanced up from her paper and snorted, then went back to reading it. I glanced at Amanda.

"Those donuts sure look good this morning," Amanda said, walking up to the counter.

"They sure do," I said. "Everything's so nice and festive looking. Stella, those Frankenstein bars look good. I think I need some of those." I pointed to the chocolate bars with Frankenstein monsters drawn on in green icing. There were round cake donuts she had frosted in orange and drawn jack-o'-lantern faces on in chocolate.

She sighed and folded her newspaper. "Is that it?"

"Yes, thanks. Stella, today's the big day," I reminded her. "We've got loads of customers coming and we need to greet them with a little more enthusiasm." I probably sounded like a Pollyanna, but I didn't care. We needed to draw more customers in, not chase them off.

She folded the newspaper over again and slapped it against her thigh. "Look kid, and yeah, to me you're still a kid, I don't have any enthusiasm left over. The last time I had enthusiasm was when we buried my mother-in-law three years ago. So take it or leave it," she said, sliding down from the stool. She went to the sink and washed her hands.

Stella was a ray of sunshine.

"I'm really glad you have a variety of Halloween themed pastries," Amanda said. "Your customers will love them." She sounded a lot more enthusiastic about it than Stella was.

"I only did it because I have leftover frosting from last year. Orange isn't a color I use very often."

"Ew," I said. "You're kidding, right?"

She shrugged. "Whatever you want, toots."

"Okay, well, how about four of the Frankenstein bars? My mother will want one and Andrea and Lisa are working today. And I agree, I'm glad you have the Halloween themed pastries. You aren't changing your mind on the Halloween season, are you?" I was hopeful, but I knew there wasn't much chance that would happen.

"No," she said and slid open the glass door in the display case.

"Great. Maybe when business picks up again, you'll change your mind," I said.

"No," she said and stuffed four Frankenstein bars into a plain white paper bag. "And for you?" she asked Amanda.

"Um, two maple boo bars would be nice."

Stella picked up another paper bag and stuck two maple bars into it. "Anything else?"

Here was my chance. I glanced at Amanda for reassurance and she nodded.

"Stella, can I ask you a question?"

"You just did. Fork over the cash for the donuts," she said and went to the cash register. I dug into my purse while she rang them up.

"Stella, do you have any idea who killed Hazel?" I asked and handed her five dollars. Our costumes were as unthreatening as they could be and I wondered if we might have chosen the wrong time to ask the question. Maybe I should have dressed as Jason from *Friday the 13th*. We might have gotten her to confess if I had brought a chain saw along.

"Why would I know that?" she asked and handed me a quarter and a dime back.

I shrugged. "It's a small town and you seem to have a lot of friends. I just thought maybe you had heard something by now. Or maybe one of your friends had heard something."

She handed me my bag. "Look. No one in this town cares who killed Hazel. The sooner you and the police figure that one out, the better. Whoever did it, did the town a favor. We are at peace now. Namaste."

I stared at her. With Stella, you never knew what you were going to get. Namaste, my foot.

"Stella, it seems like you may have had some issues with Hazel," Amanda suggested and handed her some change for her donuts.

"Ya think?" Stella asked, taking the coins and handing her the bag. "That woman was a nuisance. Like I said, whoever killed her did the town a favor."

Amanda nodded, and I suddenly felt like we might be in over our heads, but I wasn't backing down now.

"Stella, did you have something to do with Hazel's death?" I asked, as fast as I could. I took a deep breath.

The boredom never left Stella's face. Her eyes went from Amanda, then back to me again.

"Are you two out of your minds? Didn't those fancy schools you attended teach you anything?"

I glanced sideways at Amanda, but she had her eyes on Stella.

"What do you mean, Stella?" Amanda asked.

"Are you so stupid as to think I would just admit to the two of you that I killed Hazel? I mean, really? Why would I do that?" she asked. "And you—you already asked me that. What's wrong with you?" She pointed a puffy finger at me.

"So, you did kill her, but you won't admit it?" I asked.

Stella stared at me. Then she tilted her head back and roared with laughter. Amanda and I looked at each other. I wasn't sure if Stella was admitting to it or not.

The laughter went on for over a minute, and then she settled down, snorted, and wiped her eyes. "You two are just precious. No. I did not kill Hazel. She was a nuisance to be sure, but I did not kill her. Now get out of my shop. I have a newspaper to read and I'm sure some of those pesky tourists will be here any minute and then I'll have to be nice to them."

"Oh," I said and smiled. My cheeks turned pink. "So, you'll be nice to the tourists?"

"Stop it. You know I am not going to be nice to them. Now get out of here."

I nodded. "Okay Stella, well, thanks for the donuts. Sorry about the misunderstanding."

"Thanks for the laugh. College graduates." She snorted. "Funniest thing I ever heard in all my life," she said and scooted back onto the stool with her newspaper in hand.

We left the donut shop with our tails between our legs. I felt like an idiot. We should have kept our mouths shut.

"I'm not sure what to make of all that," Amanda said, opening her paper bag.

"I think we made fools of ourselves," I said. "I also think she killed Hazel."

"Do you?" Amanda asked, looking at me as we walked down the sidewalk.

I nodded. "Stella's a grumpy bully. I think she got tired of another bully picking on her and she lost it. All that back there was simply her way of distracting us."

Amanda nodded and took a bite of her donut. "These sure are fresh. I'm glad to see people are out and about already."

And they were. It wasn't eight o'clock yet, and most of the stores were still closed, but people were walking up and down the sidewalk, peering into windows. I inhaled deeply. I loved the Halloween season. There was nothing like it.

"I just hope Stella can try to be a little bit nice. I'd hate for her to run anyone off," I said and pulled a donut out of my bag.

"If she isn't nice to people, they'll just stay away from her shop and she'll be the one to suffer for it. People love coming here and they'll keep coming. I have faith in that," she said.

Amanda was right. Stella's business might suffer because of her attitude and she would have to deal with that. The rest of us would enjoy the season and do our best to make the customers happy. And if Stella had killed Hazel, I hoped it came to light as soon as possible. One thing was for sure though. The killer was not going to get away with it if I had anything to say about it. Snooping around for clues had gotten into my blood.

Chapter Sixteen

Amanda crossed the street, heading to work. Brian had already opened the coffee shop for the early birds and from the look of it, he was doing a brisk business. The weather hadn't turned cold yet, but it soon would. I had realized in previous years, that the earlier in the season the weather turned cool, the greater number of visitors would flock to Pumpkin Hollow. It seemed the cooler weather put people in the mood for the holidays, regardless of what the calendar said.

A small crowd had gathered outside of the candy shop, with several people pushing their noses against the window to see inside. I smiled. The windows would need cleaning when we closed, but I didn't care. The slower summer season was over and we would work our fingers to the bone for the next several months. I was looking forward to it.

"Excuse me," I said and squeezed between several people to get to the front door. I pulled the key out of my pocket and stuck it into the lock. "How is everyone this morning?"

"Great," a man wearing a Christmas sweater said. It appeared some people really wanted to push the holidays along.

"We are in desperate need of fudge," the woman with him spoke up and chuckled. "It might be a life or death emergency."

"Yes, candy! We need candy now!" another voice said.

I laughed. "I think I can do something about that," I said and pushed the door open. I held it as the customers streamed into the shop, then let it close softly behind the last one. It was ten minutes early, but it would make them happy. They were paying customers, and we needed every one we could get.

"I've got donuts," I mouthed to my mother as she stood behind the front counter and held up the white paper bag. She nodded, then smiled and greeted the customers. She was dressed as a 1920s flapper and she was rocking it. Mom had always looked fifteen years younger than she was and she looked absolutely darling as a flapper.

I put the bag behind the counter until we had a slow moment and Mom and the girls could eat the donuts I bought for them.

"Customers," I whispered with a grin to Andrea. She nodded and smiled.

Andrea was a sweet girl, working her way through the local junior college. I remembered my first year at college and it made me a little wistful. I had so many dreams back then. Well, my dreams had changed, but I still had them. We would restore Pumpkin Hollow to its former glory. Maybe that wasn't what I had planned when looking at career choices while in college, but it was here in front of me now and I would take it.

Andrea had dressed as a 1930s blues singer, complete with a long slinky dress. In real life, Andrea was the best singer I'd ever heard. I encouraged her to try out for one of those talent shows on TV whenever I could. She would be a sure winner.

Lisa was a high school student, and she had dressed up as a fairy. She was a cute girl with a bubbly personality and I knew the customers would love her.

I stood at the ready at the cash register and waited on people for forty-five minutes without a break in the line. When the crowd finally thinned out, I looked up to see Martha Mayes. She was dressed as a witch with a tall black pointy hat and green face makeup.

She smiled at me. "Well, that crowd was fun," she said. "I hope we see a lot more of that this season. I know the businesses could use it."

"Me too. I love to see that kind of enthusiasm this early in the season."

Andrea reached for the donut bag and handed one to my mother.

"Hello, Martha," my mother said, and sat down on a stool behind the counter. "Sorry for eating in front of you, but I'm starving. Would you like half?"

She chuckled. "That's okay, and no thank you. I've got candy on my mind." She looked into the display case.

"How have you been?" Mom asked.

She looked up at my mother. "I'm doing fine. In fact, things are just rosy these days. I love the Halloween season, and to be honest, I have a lot less work to do now."

I looked at her. "What do you mean?"

She shrugged and giggled. "Hazel Martin had me sending letters out to the homeowners all the time. All complaints have to be looked into no matter how trivial, and to be honest, she made a lot of complaints. I was constantly driving around the neighborhoods and checking things out. Then I had to send the homeowners warning letters. Personally, I don't mind if someone has a little yard decoration, or maybe their lawn gets just a bit too high. People are busy. I understand. I guess I've probably mentioned that, but I'm a little giddy about not having to work so hard. It's just a relief to not have to send out those letters. People get defensive when you tell them they're in violation of the HOA agreement."

I nodded. "I can see where people might get touchy about something like that."

"I have so much spare time during the day now, I don't know what to do with myself. I think I was doing the job of two people before and now that I only have to do the job of one, I don't know what to do," she said and laughed.

I smiled. This exchange was getting uncomfortable. "I guess things worked out for you, then." I knew Hazel was difficult, but I couldn't be happy about her death.

"I'm sorry Hazel was so difficult for you," Mom said. "I can't imagine how hard that must have been, having someone breathing down your neck all the time and making you do more work than might otherwise be necessary."

Martha sighed. "It certainly was stressful. But thankfully, that's all over."

"But a woman was murdered," I pointed out gently. It still disturbed me that so many people didn't seem to care that a murder had occurred.

"That's true. I suppose I shouldn't gloat. But my life is so much better, it's hard not to. I do hope the police figure out who killed her. I'd like to shake his or her hand." She laughed and looked into the display case again.

I gasped and stared at her. "You can't mean that."

"I'm kidding!" she said, turning back to me and cackling with laughter. The cackle made her witch's costume more realistic, but I didn't like it.

I glanced at Andrea, who stared at her wide-eyed.

"I'm sure you don't mean that," I repeated.

She shrugged. "I probably don't. I'm sorry for her family's loss. Well, I think I'd like two of those popcorn balls with black and orange sprinkles and I'll be on my way. I'm going to resist the fudge for now, but I'm sure I'll be back for some soon." She pointed a green finger with a prosthetic wart at the display of popcorn balls.

Andrea jumped up, took two popcorn balls from the display case and put them into wax paper bags, then into a larger Halloween printed bag and handed the bag to her. I rang Martha up and took her money. We all watched her as she exited the shop, waving at us as she left.

"I don't get that," Andrea said. "I didn't really know Hazel, but even if she was a terrible person, I can't imagine being happy someone killed her."

"Me either," I said. "And I did know her and didn't particularly like her. I still can't get over people acting that way."

"We need to make more fudge, I think," Mom said with a sigh. "We've already sold five pounds of it."

"That's good news," I said. "I hope business really turns around this year."

"Did you get the city website made?" Andrea asked. Her parents owned a craft shop, and they depended on the Halloween season as much as we did.

"I'm almost done. I've been working on it every night after work. I can hardly wait to show it off." I picked up a box of Halloween decorations that still needed to be put up and set it on the counter to look through.

"I'm glad you came home, Mia," Mom said. "I think ideas around here became old and stale a long time ago and everyone eventually gave up on the town."

"Me, too," I agreed. More customers came through the door and I smiled at them. "I'll make the fudge for you." The decorations could wait. We needed more candy to sell.

I headed to the kitchen and grabbed a hair net and an apron and put them on. The kitchen always smelled like chocolate no matter what we were making, and I inhaled deeply. I loved the smell. I weighed out the sugar and put it into the large pan on the stove. One large batch of fudge coming up.

After checking on what we already had made, I decided on a large batch of chocolate and another of peanut butter. The other flavors would probably hold out for the rest of the day. I turned the heat on low beneath the saucepan, remembering when my grandmother would make the fudge on Saturday mornings. She had been gone more than ten years, but I still missed her. I thought she would approve of my efforts to save the town and would have jumped right in to help me if she had still been here.

Chapter Seventeen

SATURDAY AFTERNOON I had the fun of judging the pumpkin carving contest. The contest was one of the oldest traditions in Pumpkin Hollow and I felt honored to be chosen as judge. It didn't hurt that the merchants got to vote and since we'd just had the meeting to save the Halloween season, it was a cinch that I'd be chosen.

Tables had been set up near the gazebo at the park and I sat on the step, waiting for the bell to ring signaling the end of the contest. On one side were the adults, who were allowed sharp instruments. "Cut at your own peril" was the motto for the adults. On the other side were the kids, broken down by age groups. They had colored markers, paints, glitter, and stickers available to do their artwork.

I wasn't sure how I would pick winners from the kids' groups. I didn't want to make anyone sad by not picking their pumpkin. I looked up when a shadow fell across me.

"Hey Mia, are you ready to judge the jack-o'-lanterns?" Ethan asked.

I smiled. "I'm as ready as I'll ever be. I do worry about disappointing the kids though. There's only a first through third place winner for each age group and we have about ten kids per age group."

"I'd worry more about disappointing the adults. They have sharp implements and they look pretty serious about the whole carving thing," he said and sat beside me.

I laughed. "On second thought, you might be right. Will you stick around to protect me?" As soon as it was out of my mouth, I regretted it. I didn't want him to think I was a damsel in distress that needed saving.

He chuckled. "I do come armed, so I guess I could stick around."

I smiled at him. "I'm glad. I'm also glad you're working on finding Hazel's killer. Someone else might not work as hard to find her killer. Seems a lot of people don't care that she died."

"All I'm really doing is gathering information and following up with people. I don't know how close we are to solving the case, but I know those higher up in the department have their eyes on a couple of people. But we still need more time before we make an arrest."

I nodded. "Would those people happen to be Stella Moretti or Martha Mayes?" I asked.

"I'm not at liberty to say. Are their attitudes still bothering you?" He tilted his head and cocked an eyebrow at me.

I nodded. "I guess I shouldn't let it get to me. I guess it's because they're so callous about the whole thing. Mr. Gott, too, I guess. Actually, I guess on that basis alone, I could come up with a whole list of people that could be suspects," I said and chuckled. "I know Hazel was a pain, but it seems like people could be just a tad more sorry about her being killed like she was."

He nodded. "Hazel didn't mind making enemies, that's for sure. But like I said, I can't divulge that kind of information."

"Maybe you should question all of them again? Maybe they'd break if the police keep questioning them."

He chuckled. "Do we need to drag them into a room and shine a bare light bulb into their eyes and grill them?"

I smiled. "You know what I mean. It's not just that they don't care that she died; it's that they're happy she died. Thrilled, even. It makes me very suspicious."

"I'll be asking a few people some more questions. It won't hurt anything. Unless they complain to the chief. He doesn't like complaints."

"Seriously? It's a murder investigation," I said.

He nodded. "It's a small town, and he likes things to run smoothly."

I shook my head at him. The bell went off, and I stood up. "Everyone needs to stop what they're doing," I announced. I had borrowed a bullhorn from the police department, and I was really feeling like I had some power now.

I heard a couple of groans as markers and carving tools were put down.

"Thank you," I said and put the bullhorn down. I looked at Ethan. "Want to help?"

"Sure," he said, and we strolled along the tables of carved pumpkins.

I had a clipboard with paper to write notes on. The youngest group was the three to four-year-old age group. The pumpkins had messy paint drips, coloring out of the lines, and a few well-placed stickers to look like lips.

"What's your pumpkin's name?" I asked a little blond haired boy.

He stuck his chest out and smiled at me. "Harold. He likes to eat jelly beans."

I laughed. "Well, Harold is very fancy looking," I told him. Harold had a black sticker eye patch and some plastic gemstones glued in his mouth and had a rakish tilt to his head.

We walked along, looking at each pumpkin, and I made notes on the paper attached to my clipboard. The kids would all get cotton candy as consolation prizes, so it wouldn't be terrible if they didn't get the big prize; a trick or treat bag filled with candy, donated by yours truly.

The adult winners would get tickets to the corn maze and hayrides. Adult non-winners didn't get a consolation prize, but we figured they were adults and they could handle it. After Ethan and I made the tour of the carving tables, we moved off to the side to consult on the winners.

"I am really liking Harold," Ethan said. "He's a striking pirate."

I giggled. "I like him, too. It's those plastic gemstones in his teeth."

In the end, we selected the best possible winners. In the adult group, we had a pirate, a witch, and a haunted house scene. I suspected these people had done this quite a few times as there weren't any mistakes in the cuts on the surfaces of the pumpkins.

For the kids, we chose Harold, a turkey, and a puppy in the three to four-year-old group and in the older age groups, we had scarecrows, witches, and mummies.

I picked up the bullhorn and made the announcements of winners to polite applause. Ethan stood next to me and handed out the prizes.

"Well, that was an enjoyable afternoon," Ethan said when we finished up.

"I had a lot of fun. I'm glad I moved home," I said. I hesitated a moment. It was the first time I had admitted that to myself. Smiling, I picked up a cardboard box, headed to one of the carving tables and pushed the pumpkin seeds and membranes into the box. Ethan went to the other side of the table with his own box and did the same.

"I'm glad you came home, too," he said as he pushed a large pile into his box. I glanced at him but didn't say anything.

"So, has anyone from Hazel's family contacted the police?" I asked, changing the subject.

"The next of kin was notified when she died, but I haven't heard anything else. Have you noticed anyone next door, maybe going through things in the house?"

I shook my head. "No. I kind of expected someone to show up. I imagine they'll sell the house. Unless a family member moves in."

"Yeah, no telling. But I bet whoever your new neighbor turns out to be, they'll be easier to get along with than the former one," he said with a wicked grin.

"Stop," I said, narrowing my eyes at him. I grinned. "She was a perfectly delightful neighbor."

"Liar."

I laughed. "I am a liar," I admitted.

We cleared off the tables and then wiped them down. The pumpkin carving contest had been a success. We just needed a few more weekend events like this one and we would be on our way to a more prosperous Halloween season.

Chapter Eighteen

"I DECLARE THE BEGINNING of the Halloween season a success," I said, turning the lock on the candy shop door. A few people still milled about on the sidewalk, but most had gone home for the day. I had forgotten how exhausting the season was. Every bone in my body ached.

"I agree," Mom said, wiping down the front counter. "We sold a lot of fudge."

Our two part-time employees, Andrea and Lisa, scurried about the shop cleaning up. I was glad we had hired them. They were making things a lot easier on Mom and me. Mostly Mom, since she did the bulk of the candy making.

"I think things will really turn around this year," I said, picking up the broom and sweeping. "And If I don't fall asleep as soon as I get home, I think I can finish up the website. I'm pretty tired though."

"That would be great," Lisa said, straightening a display of boxed candy pumpkins. "I bet it helps the town a lot."

I nodded. I would do whatever it took to save the Halloween season. We finished cleaning up as quickly as we could and left for the evening. The morning would come all too early and I needed a shower and sleep after I worked for a bit on the website.

MOM PULLED INTO OUR driveway and parked the car. My head was resting on the seat back and my eyes were closed. I had felt myself slipping into sleep and shook myself when she turned the engine off.

"I am so tired," I mumbled and sat up, opening my eyes. It was twilight outside. The days were getting shorter and cooler. Leaves were falling from the trees and I could hardly wait for sweater and boot weather, not to mention warm, cozy pumpkin spice lattes. I loved the fall more than any other time of year.

"I'm pretty beat, too," Mom said. "I hope your father made something for dinner. Otherwise, I think a sandwich might be in order."

"I'm fine with a sandwich, I don't need anything fancy. I just want to take a shower and go to bed," I said and opened the car door.

I thought the website might have to wait after all. I either needed to exercise to build up my stamina, or I needed to sleep more to keep up with the season. I wasn't sure which.

"I made dinner," Dad called as we walked in the door. "Pot roast, potatoes, and carrots."

"You don't know how happy that makes me," Mom said. "I married the best man ever."

"Yes, you did. It'll be another forty-five minutes until it's ready though," he said from the living room.

I could smell the pot roast and my stomach growled. "I'm going upstairs. Call me when we're ready to eat?" I called to whoever cared.

"You bet," Dad replied.

I trudged up the stairs, wishing we lived in a single level house. My thigh muscles screamed at me and I wasn't sure why they were so tired. It wasn't like I had run a marathon or anything.

I pushed open the door to my room and lay down to stare at the ceiling. I had forgotten to turn on the light on my way to the bed, but I was too tired to get up and turn it on. My laptop was on my bedside table, and I considered opening it up and working on the website, but my eyes were tired. I closed them and lay still, not caring if I fell asleep before dinner.

As I lay there, I became aware of a steady crunching sound. Once my mind picked up on it, I couldn't let it go. My eyes opened, and the sleepiness was suddenly gone. Where was that coming from?

I felt a light breeze blow across my arms and face and I realized my window was halfway open. The room had been stuffy the night before and I forgot to close it when I got up this morning. I sat up and then went to the window. The sound was coming from outside so I pushed the window all the way open and peered out.

Hazel's house and Mr. Gott's house were single level houses and I had a view into both back yards. Both houses were dark, but Mr. Gott had a light on in his back yard. I leaned out a little further and I could just see him working in his yard. He was digging a hole. I wondered why he would dig a hole this late in the evening. Each time he stuck the shovel into the ground, I heard the crunching sound.

I stood up straight. It was late to be working in the yard. I couldn't imagine what he was doing. Then I thought about his little dog, Millie. She was getting old, and I wondered if she had passed away. Was Mr. Gott burying her? Should I offer to help him? My body was aching and my mind was tired. I sighed. Poor thing. Millie was all he had.

I headed out of the room and down the stairs, still dressed in my Dorothy costume. Thankfully, in this town, no one would look at me strangely. My mother had brought home some of the leftover fudge, so I went to the kitchen and wrapped up a large piece for Mr. Gott. It might make him feel a little better.

"What are you doing, Mia?" Mom asked from the living room.

"I'm going to take some fudge to Mr. Gott," I answered. I picked up a Halloween decorated paper bag and slipped the wrapped fudge into it, folding down the top of the bag. "I'll be back in a few minutes."

"Okay, dear. Don't be too late. Dinner will be ready soon."

I headed out the front door and over to Mr. Gott's, crossing over Hazel's lawn. I wouldn't have dared do it if she were still alive. I'd never hear the end of it and we would get a letter from the homeowners association.

It was completely dark outside now and Mr. Gott's front porch light was off. I pressed the doorbell, hoping he could hear it from the backyard.

When he didn't answer, I pressed it again. There was still no answer, so I pounded on the door. Finally, I heard shuffling footsteps nearing the door.

The deadbolt slid back in its track and the doorknob jiggled, followed by the door opening.

"Good evening, Mr. Gott," I said, hoping I wouldn't frighten him by stopping by after dark. "It's me, Mia. I brought you some fudge." I held up the paper bag with its bright Halloween print. The orange and green colors nearly glowed in the dark.

Mr. Gott peered over his silver wire-framed glasses at the bag. He smiled and looked at me but didn't take the bag. "Good evening, Mia. That was thoughtful of you. I was hoping you'd stop by. Why don't you come in?"

"Sure," I said. I wasn't sure why he had hoped I would stop by, unless Millie really had died, and he needed some help in burying her. "But I can only stay for a minute. My dad is making dinner and it will be ready soon."

He opened the door wider and turned around, shuffling back inside. I followed him into the darkened house and wondered when he would turn a light on. It was darker inside the house than it was outside, and I willed my eyes to adjust, hoping I didn't trip over anything.

"Mr. Gott, do you have a light?" I asked when my leg grazed something in the dark.

"What? Oh, yes," he said and flipped a switch that illuminated the living room.

There was a footstool near where my leg grazed something. The living room hadn't changed since I was a little girl. The old frilly shaded lamps still sat on the maple end tables and the sofas were still covered in plastic. I smiled when Millie trotted into the room. She came to me and sniffed my leg. Then she sat down and looked up at me hopefully. Millie was a cross between a schnauzer and a Chihuahua and had loads of personality. Her gray and black wiry hair needed a trim, but her bright eyes begged me for what was in the bag I held.

"Sorry, Millie, but dogs can't have fudge," I said and I bent down, patting her head.

Mr. Gott continued into the kitchen and I followed after him with Millie on my heels. The kitchen was done in a 1980s country cow theme that Mrs. Gott had loved when she had been alive.

"Did you get to go downtown for the opening of the Halloween season?" I asked Mr. Gott. "It was a good one. There were lots of people and that's good for the town."

"Halloween season?" he asked without looking at me. "Bah!"

I sighed, hoping he would come around. "Well, it's good for the town."

Mr. Gott stopped and turned toward me. His face was expressionless, and he looked at me without answering. Then he turned and went to the kitchen counter and opened a drawer.

Chapter Nineteen

"I DON'T LIKE THE HALLOWEEN season," Mr. Gott said, rummaging through the drawer. "I told you that. We'd all be better off if they put an end to that shameful practice. Imagine, grown people dressing up in costumes!"

I tried to come up with a response, but some people would never change and I decided not to argue with him.

Mr. Gott turned toward me and I gasped.

"Mr. Gott, what are you doing?" I asked, staring at him.

He held a revolver in his hand and pointed it at me.

"I said I don't like the Halloween season," he repeated. "Aren't you listening? Why do you persist in forcing that darned celebration on us, honest, peaceable folks? It's a nuisance, and people who like the Halloween season are also a nuisance."

My mind shut down momentarily as I tried to process what was happening, and I went numb. I was aware of the paper bag of fudge in my hand and Millie sniffing at my heels again, but little else.

"What are you doing with that?" I couldn't tear my eyes away from the gun.

"Stella Moretti said you were working very hard on keeping the Halloween season going. She said you were organizing meetings and making a website to get more people to come to Pumpkin Hollow. I do not like it. Stella Moretti does not like it, and neither does anyone else. You should not have come back to Pumpkin Hollow, Mia," he said slowly. "I like you, but you're making life miserable for a lot of people. Me included."

My eyes went to his. He didn't seem himself. "Mr. Gott, I think we can talk about this rationally."

"I don't mean to be unkind, but we have some unpleasant business to attend to. I don't have time to talk," he said and motioned with the gun to the back door. "Come."

"Why?" I asked. I didn't really want an answer; my mind was just trying to process what was happening.

"Put the fudge down. I always did like your mother's fudge." He motioned to the kitchen counter. "I wonder if she'll make any more after you're gone?"

I reached over and put the bag down, trying to make my mind work.

"Mr. Gott, this is ridiculous," I said. "We need to talk this out like rational people."

"We don't have time to talk. Now, come," he said again and motioned toward the back door.

I put one foot in front of the other and moved toward the door. When I got to it, I stopped.

"Now, push it open and go down the steps," he said, stepping up close behind me and put the gun barrel against my back. "You know how to do that, don't you?"

I did as I was told.

Stall.

"Mr. Gott, my parents are expecting me home in a minute. My dad made roast beef for dinner. Would you like to eat with us? It smells really good."

"Roast beef. I'm sure it would be nice," he said, "but we have business to attend to."

"What kind of business?" I asked. It was then I saw the hole he had been digging. Seeing it up close, I realized it was far too big for little Millie. It wasn't what I would call human-sized, but if a person's legs were bent, they could fit. If they weren't too large. My stomach churned.

"Important business," he said, following close behind me. I felt the gun press into my back and I stopped breathing for a moment.

"Mr. Gott, I don't understand. If you don't like the Halloween season, there will be a vote at the next city council meeting. You can voice your opinion then," I explained. I swallowed. "Mr. Gott, did you kill Hazel?" I had nothing to lose by asking it, and I already knew the answer anyway.

"Yes," he said, but didn't elaborate as we walked toward the hole.

"Why?" I asked. "I don't think she was a fan of the Halloween season. She would have been on your side."

"She hated the Halloween season. If she had lived, she probably would have been the person most likely to get it stopped. Sadly, she died."

"But why? Why did you kill her?" I asked. My head swam with what was happening and I had to breathe deeply to keep from passing out.

We stopped near the edge of the hole and I turned toward him, frantically trying to come up with a plan.

"She was always complaining about my grass, Millie's barking, my flag. Everything bothered her. I didn't mean to do it. We got into an argument about the height of my grass and I accidentally pushed her. She fell down the steps at the front of her house. Her head hit the concrete, and she didn't move. Fortunately for me, all the neighbors, including you and your parents, were at work. What a wonderful stroke of good luck for me."

"You could tell the police what happened. It was an accident and I'm sure they'll understand," I said helpfully.

He smiled at me, but the smile didn't reach his eyes. "I suppose I could have called them and told them she tripped. They would have believed me. But it seemed like such a fine idea to turn her into a scarecrow; something she detested. So I did. It would be too late now to tell the police Hazel had an accident. They'd never believe me. Did I ever tell you how much I hated her? Always have. She was a busy body and she caused me to lose my job back in 1966. Told my boss I was stealing from the bank deposits. I wasn't, but there were some missing funds, so it was convenient for them to blame me."

I nodded. "Okay, well, what do I have to do with what she did in 1966? I've never complained about you or Millie. I'm not following any of this."

"You've been asking people about Hazel's death. People have told me you have. Stella at the bakery said you even accused her of killing Hazel. And then you asked me about it. Obviously I wanted to keep it quiet. I didn't want anyone to find out, but you just kept asking. I also want the Halloween season stopped and there you are, trying so hard to save it. So, I figured if I did away with you, it would solve two problems at once. I'm sorry, but I have no choice." He looked at me sadly, shaking his head. Then he brightened. "You coming over here this evening is another wonderful stroke of good luck for me. I wasn't sure how I would get you over here, but you just showed up as if you knew I was expecting you."

I stared at him. He was mad as a hatter. "Someone will hear the gunshot," I pointed out. "And my parents are expecting me home."

"It's a small gun, its not very loud. Everyone has their television going this time of night," he said, sounding reasonable. "And no one will think to check the backyard of a sweet old man like me. Your parents will think you wandered off and that one of those pesky tourists did something to you. At which point, I will remind everyone that I said they should quit having the Halloween season. You never know what kind of people it will attract to this town."

"I told my parents I was coming over here. They'll check here first," I pointed out.

"And I'll tell them you never showed up. Like I said, the police are never going to suspect a sweet old man like me," he said with a grin. "Once you get to be a certain age, people automatically dismiss you. It used to bother me, but now I rather enjoy it. It leaves me free to do almost anything I please."

"This is ridiculous, Mr. Gott. No one will believe you."

He shrugged. "Even if I were caught, life in prison isn't much of a threat at my age. But I doubt anyone will suspect me. So you see, Mia, I have nothing to lose."

I took a deep breath. It was now or never. I hit his hand that was holding the gun and it flew off to the side and bounced once on the grass.

"You!" he said and swore under his breath. He bent and reached for the gun. I grabbed him by the shoulders and threw him into the hole he had dug for me and I ran for the house.

I wondered if he might be able to get out of the hole and grab the gun before I could get all the way through his house and I wished I had stopped to pick it up. What was I thinking? Fear had me in a stranglehold and I just wanted out of there. I sprinted for the back door and ran through the house. I wanted to scream, but I couldn't get enough air into my lungs.

Millie ran after me as I ran past her and I was out his front door in less than a minute and sprinting across his front lawn, and then Hazel's lawn. Once inside my front door, I slammed it shut and leaned against it, breathing hard. I felt like I was about to faint, so I crouched down in the foyer and gasped for air.

"Mia, what is it?" Mom asked, getting out of her chair.

"Dial 911. Mr. Gott tried to kill me," I gasped.

"What?" she asked, staring at me.

I looked at her with tears in my eyes.

"Please," I whispered.

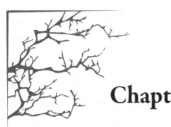

Chapter Twenty

I sat on the bottom step of our staircase with a blanket wrapped around me. The police had taken Mr. Gott away, and Millie sat at my feet, resting her head on my shoe. Mom had brought me a cup of cocoa, but I had hardly touched it. The front door was open and I could still see the red and blue lights flashing on one of the patrol cars parked at the curb.

A figure walked toward me in the dark and I braced myself. I'd had all the excitement I could stand for one day.

Ethan walked into view, his jaw set hard. He was dressed in jeans and a t-shirt. "Hey, Mia," he said gently.

I nodded at him. "Hey."

He sat down on the step next to me and reached out and scratched Millie's head. "Are you okay, Mia?"

I nodded, but didn't look at him.

"The other officers told me what happened. I'm sorry."

"Thanks," I said quietly. "I can't believe Mr. Gott would try to kill me. I always thought he was a nice man. I couldn't have been more wrong. He's seemed a little off since I moved back, but I didn't think much of it."

"I'm pretty surprised, too," he said. "I don't think anyone suspected him in Hazel's murder."

"This whole thing is crazy. He attacked Hazel because she made him angry, but I still don't get why he would dress her up as a scarecrow. He said it seemed like a fine idea. What does that even mean?"

"He told the arresting officer he thought it would give the Halloween season a bad name and the mayor would stop the celebration. That almost worked."

"It still might," I said and took a sip of my now cold cocoa.

"Let's hope not. He also said he was sorry he had done it and that he should have just called the police and told us she fell," he said. "That probably would have been the smarter move. We would have believed it was an accident then."

"Is he still saying it was an accident?" I asked and reached down and scratched Millie's ear.

"Yes, he still maintains it was an accident. He said dressing her up as a scarecrow was an afterthought. It'll be up to a judge to decide, but I think we both know it isn't true."

"He said he accidentally pushed her. Maybe it was an accident, and his mind snapped when he realized she was dead." I shrugged, trying to reason this thing out. "I guess it was convenient to use her death to try to stop the Halloween season from continuing. I can't believe someone hated it that much. Trying to kill me wasn't an accident, though."

He nodded. "He said he was tired of the crowds and the traffic. He also said he was embarrassed that grown people dressed up in costumes," Ethan said with a chuckle. "He could have just stayed home. It would have made things easier for everyone."

I shook my head and looked at him. "I've never been so scared in my life. I mean, he just went out into the back yard and dug a grave for me. He was going to shoot me like it was no big deal." I trembled at the thought. "He even thought he'd get away with it without anyone questioning him."

"There's no telling about some people. I'm sorry you went through that. How did you get away?"

"In my sophomore year of college, there were several assaults on female students on campus, so the school offered self-defense courses. I took one, but once they caught the perpetrator, I never thought I would use those skills. Was I ever wrong. Not that it took much. I just knocked the gun out of his hand and ran. It's a good thing he was elderly, otherwise he might have put up more of a fight."

"It's a good thing you took the class. It probably gave you more confidence than you would have had otherwise, and things could have turned out very differently."

"To be honest, it wasn't that much of a challenge. He lost his grip on the gun pretty easily." I chuckled bitterly. Mr. Gott's plans for me had been thwarted, but I was still angry that he thought he could get away with it.

"I'm glad of that," he said softly.

I shook my head. "For the first few minutes, my mind was a blank. It wasn't until the last minute that I remembered the instructor saying not to go anywhere with someone who had a gun. He said we'd die for sure if we did. Something inside me made me reach over and knock that gun out of his hand. I didn't even think."

"I'm just glad you're okay," he said again and reached out and gave my shoulder a squeeze.

"Thanks, me too," I said. "We've got Millie here if Mr. Gott's relatives don't claim her."

"Will you keep her if they don't?"

"Probably," I said. "She's pretty old and I've known her all her life. She was a puppy when Mr. Gott brought her home. Besides, she's never tried to shoot me. I can't hold it against her that her owner tried to."

Ethan chuckled. "Let's hope she stays on the right side of the law."

I laughed. "I'll keep an eye on her."

"I'm really glad you came back to Pumpkin Hollow." He looked at me intently.

My stomach did a flip-flop and I smiled at Ethan. Having Ethan sitting next to me made me feel safe. I wasn't sure I wanted a relationship, or if Ethan did, but he had been on my mind a lot since he had shown up to investigate Hazel's death. We had the same goal of saving the town and we got along well. We would have to wait and see how things turned out.

I hoped Mr. Gott got the help he needed. At his age I wasn't sure he'd ever see freedom again, but that might not have been a bad thing. He had lost that something on the inside that keeps people from killing other people, and once lost, I wasn't sure it could be gotten back.

I wasn't more tired now than I had been before I made a mad dash to safety, and I wasn't sure how I would get up and go to work the next day, but I knew I would. Staying home with my freshly dug grave just two houses away wasn't an option. Besides, we had a Halloween season to save. It might take me the entire season to do it, but it was something I was committed to doing.

The End

Sneak Peek

Murderously Sweet

A Pumpkin Hollow Mystery, book 2

Chapter One

"Let the murders begin!"

My head jerked around to see who had shouted. Two teenagers ran toward the entrance to the corn maze, laughing and screaming. I smiled and breathed in deeply. Everything was fine. Hazel Martin's killer was behind bars and the Halloween season would go on as planned.

"You aren't scared of a little corn maze, are you?" a voice said close to my ear.

I squealed and jumped, spinning around to face whoever had spoken.

"Ethan!" I exclaimed. My hair blew across my face and I tucked it back behind my ear.

"Whoa. Sorry, I didn't mean to scare you," he said, holding the flat of his palms toward me. "Sorry, Mia." He grinned as he said it, making me think he didn't mean it.

I rolled my eyes. "Thanks a lot, Ethan. My blood pressure just shot through the roof."

He grinned. "Scaredy cat."

"I am not scared, Mr. Police Officer. I was just taking in a lovely sight," I said, motioning to all the people wandering around the haunted farmhouse with its two frighteningly fun mazes. The three horse-drawn hayrides were just pulling away from the barn and were filled to capacity. "Isn't it lovely?"

"It certainly is," he agreed, looking toward the mazes.

The haunted farmhouse was one of the most popular attractions Pumpkin Hollow had to offer. The tamer maze was made of bales of straw that boasted wooden pumpkin and ghost cutouts. It was well loved by families with small children.

The not so tame maze was made from cornstalks. After the corn was harvested and the stalks dried out, trails were plowed through the field. Lurking in its shadows were Freddy Kruger, Michael Myers of horror movie fame, and an assortment of generic ghouls and goblins, ready to jump out and scare the brave souls that dared enter.

"I was worried we might not have large crowds after what happened to Hazel," I said. When Hazel Martin was murdered earlier in the season, the business owners worried it would scare tourists off.

Ethan nodded, his blond hair falling across his forehead. He pushed it back. "It is a pretty wonderful sight. Hazel Martin's murder didn't run off the tourists after all."

Pumpkin Hollow was a small town that boasted a Halloween theme year-round. But the Halloween season was from Labor Day to mid-November and the town relied on this season to bring in revenue to keep it going.

"It's a huge relief," I said, pushing back my long hair. It was medium brown and I wondered if I should color it orange or green to celebrate the season.

"Are you going into the corn maze?" he asked. Ethan was a police officer but was off duty and wearing jeans and a black t-shirt. I had to tilt my head up to look him in the eye.

"Maybe," I said, looking at the entrance.

"You're not scared, are you? Because if you are scared, there's always the straw maze. I'm sure the kindergartners won't mind you joining them."

I narrowed my eyes at him. "Listen, smarty-pants, I'm not afraid of the corn maze. It's just kind of crowded in there right now."

He chuckled. "I haven't seen very many people go in there. It's pretty dark now and the ghouls will come out from the shadows. But don't be chicken. They don't bite that hard."

I sighed and crossed my arms over my chest, giving him the eye. It had been years since I had been in the corn maze. Ten years to be exact. October of my senior year of high school, I had gone through the corn maze with a group of friends that included a boyfriend who I had felt I was on the verge of breaking up with. The corn maze sealed the deal when he hid behind some corn stalks and jumped out at me, squirting fake blood on my face and blouse. Yeah. That did it for me. I went home with one of my friends and left him behind, refusing to answer his phone calls.

Ethan tilted his head and looked at me questioningly.

"Fine. Let's go through the corn maze," I said. What could go wrong? I knew most of the actors that played the scary creeps hiding in the maze. It wasn't like they would hurt me.

"I knew you'd do it," he said. "If you get too scared, you can hold my hand."

I snorted as we headed toward the entrance. "I don't think that will be necessary."

Ethan and I hadn't been friends in school. In fact, in the seventh grade he had started a rumor that I had spiders in my hair. Try living that one down in a Halloween town.

Ethan took out his wallet for the entrance fee and I stuck my hand in my pocket for the money I had stowed there so I wouldn't have to carry my purse around.

"I got it," he said over his shoulder as he handed the zombie at the entrance the money.

"Oh, you don't have to do that," I insisted. It felt a little awkward to have someone I really didn't know very well pay my entrance fee. I had been away from Pumpkin Hollow for ten years, earning three master's degrees at the University of Michigan, and had lost contact with most of the kids I knew in high school. After ten years of studying, I still didn't know what I wanted to do with my life and here I was, back in the small town I thought I had left behind for good.

"I said I got it," he said glancing over his shoulder.

"Thank you," I said. There was no use arguing with him when the police officer in him came out.

We could hear screams coming from the corn maze and if I was being truthful, I felt a little nervous about the whole thing. It was dumb. There was nothing to worry about, but having someone jump out at you with a chainsaw can be scary even if you know they won't actually hurt you.

As we walked down the first path, I heard a growl coming from the stalks of corn. I stepped a little closer to Ethan.

He chuckled. "I must have left my dog out. He won't hurt you, though."

I took a deep breath and smiled. It was all in fun. Right?

"What's that?" I asked, pointing at a hulking figure in the shadows up ahead.

"Let's go find out," he said with a grin.

There were dim lights put up in the corners of the maze, but large portions of the maze were in complete darkness. I kept my eye on the dark figure as we approached it.

"Hey buddy, you lost?" Ethan asked it.

The thing started groaning and swaying back and forth. It was covered in a black cloak and a blank black mask covered its face. I pressed against the walls of the corn maze, hoping it wouldn't reach out and grab me.

"Let's go."

The groans got louder. Ethan laughed again and stepped around it.

As I passed, it reached out and took hold of my wrist. I screamed, jerking my arm away from it. The figure dressed in black screamed along with me, and then broke out in loud cackles.

I broke into a trot and headed up the path. Ethan brought up the rear, still laughing.

"Don't talk to strangers, Mia. It's stranger danger 101," he called to me.

"Yeah, thanks for the advice, Ethan," I said, trying to control the fear. It was dumb to be scared of this place, but I couldn't help it. I stopped and let him catch up to me. "This was a bad idea."

"It will be fine," he said when he caught up. "I won't let them get you. This is what the Halloween season is all about."

"I prefer the family-friendly entertainment," I said. We walked on, turning a corner. A green goblin jumped out at me and I screamed again and ran, dodging him as I passed.

I heard footsteps running after me and I glanced over my shoulder. It was Ethan and he was still laughing. I slowed to a stop and turned toward him, hands on my hips.

"What's so funny? I don't see anything to laugh about," I huffed.

"Honestly, Mia, I didn't think this was going to be so entertaining." He bent over and put his hands on his thighs, still laughing and trying to catch his breath.

"I'm glad someone is enjoying themselves," I said and turned around and headed down the path. Two teenagers pushed past me, laughing and screaming, and ran up ahead.

"I'm sorry, Mia, you are correct. This is no laughing matter," Ethan said, trying to sound serious. He straightened up and caught up to me.

I smirked. "Whatever, Mr. Officer. Laugh all you want. I'm going to find a hole in the side of this maze to escape through and get out of here."

"You don't want to do that. You'll miss all the excitement. We haven't seen Freddy yet."

"I can do without seeing Freddy. I should have trusted my instincts and done the straw bale maze."

"The first rule of avoiding assault is to trust your instincts," he informed me. "You should have listened to yourself."

I snorted and we walked side by side down the path. The hair on the back of my neck stood on end as I squinted my eyes in the dark. There was a lot of screaming going on and I really did wonder if there was a way out of this thing without going all the way to the end. The path we were following dead-ended in the dark and we turned back.

"How do we get out of this thing?" I asked him.

"If you want your freedom, you've got to earn it," he said. "That's why they call it a maze. It will be amazing if you live through it."

"Ha ha," I said.

A mummy with bloody bandages jumped out at me and I screamed and ran again. I let Ethan catch up with me and we walked on while I searched for an exit. The air was humid inside the maze with the evening turning warmer than expected, and I wished I hadn't worn a light windbreaker. All the running I was doing was making me sweat.

We turned another corner and came face to face with a chainsaw-wielding madman with a white-painted and scarred face and red hair. He pulled the start pulley and revved the chainsaw at us. I screamed and ran down a path leading away from him.

My senses told me I was headed the opposite direction from the exit, but I didn't care. I was done with things jumping out at me and I was going to make my own exit in the side of the maze if need be.

"Mia, slow down!" I heard Ethan call.

It was fully dark now and there weren't any lights down this corridor. I kept running. At the last moment, I realized I was going to hit a wall. I tried to pull up, but hit the cornstalks, tripped over something on the ground, and sprawled onto the hard-packed path.

My head spun and I gasped for air. I tried to inhale, but my lungs didn't seem to work after the fall knocked the air out of them.

"Mia, are you okay?" Ethan asked, catching up and kneeling beside me. He was breathing hard and put one hand on my shoulder.

I looked up at him, still trying to get some air in. After what seemed like a very long moment, my breath caught and I inhaled. I willed myself not to cry with the effort of breathing.

"Mia, are you okay?" he asked again.

I nodded and forced myself to smile, pushing myself up onto my elbows. I rolled over and winced.

"My ankle hurts," I said, sitting up and trying to pull my leg closer so I could get a look at it.

"Be careful, it might be broken," Ethan said, and took his phone out of his pocket. He turned on the flashlight app and shined it onto my ankle. "Tell me if I'm hurting you."

I winced as he gently slid the cuff of my jeans up away from my ankle. "Ow," I said.

"Sorry," he said. "Lie down, it might make it easier. I know a little first aid, but we may need to call an ambulance if you can't walk out of here."

"Oh, no, don't do that," I said, and lay down on the ground. I could just imagine EMTs having to drag a gurney back through the maze to bring me out while everyone gathered around to watch.

"It's starting to swell a little," he said as he ran gentle fingers over my ankle.

I gasped. "Ow."

"Sorry. Sit up and let's see if you can put any weight on it," he said and put his hand out for me to take.

I took a deep breath and glanced to my left before sitting up again. That was when I screamed.

Buy Murderously Sweet on Amazon:

https://www.amazon.com/Murderously-Sweet-Pumpkin-Hollow-Mystery-ebook/dp/B0754M279Z/

Sign up to receive my newsletter for updates on new releases and sales:

https://www.subscribepage.com/kathleen-suzette

Follow me on Facebook:

https://www.facebook.com/Kathleen-Suzette-Kate-Bell-authors-759206390932120

Books by Kathleen Suzette:

A Rainey Daye Cozy Mystery Series

Clam Chowder and a Murder
A Rainey Daye Cozy Mystery, book 1
A Short Stack and a Murder
A Rainey Daye Cozy Mystery, book 2
Cherry Pie and a Murder
A Rainey Daye Cozy Mystery, book 3
Barbecue and a Murder
A Rainey Daye Cozy Mystery, book 4
Birthday Cake and a Murder
A Rainey Daye Cozy Mystery, book 5
Hot Cider and a Murder
A Rainey Daye Cozy Mystery, book 6
Roast Turkey and a Murder
A Rainey Daye Cozy Mystery, book 7
Gingerbread and a Murder
A Rainey Daye Cozy Mystery, book 8
Fish Fry and a Murder
A Rainey Daye Cozy Mystery, book 9
Cupcakes and a Murder
A Rainey Daye Cozy Mystery, book 10
Lemon Pie and a Murder
A Rainey Daye Cozy Mystery, book 11
Pasta and a Murder
A Rainey Daye Cozy Mystery, book 12

Chocolate Cake and a Murder
A Rainey Daye Cozy Mystery, book 13
Pumpkin Spice Donuts and a Murder
A Rainey Daye Cozy Mystery, book 14

A Pumpkin Hollow Mystery Series

Candy Coated Murder
A Pumpkin Hollow Mystery, book 1
Murderously Sweet
A Pumpkin Hollow Mystery, book 2
Chocolate Covered Murder
A Pumpkin Hollow Mystery, book 3
Death and Sweets
A Pumpkin Hollow Mystery, book 4
Sugared Demise
A Pumpkin Hollow Mystery, book 5
Confectionately Dead
A Pumpkin Hollow Mystery, book 6
Hard Candy and a Killer
A Pumpkin Hollow Mystery, book 7
Candy Kisses and a Killer
A Pumpkin Hollow Mystery, book 8
Terminal Taffy
A Pumpkin Hollow Mystery, book 9
Fudgy Fatality
A Pumpkin Hollow Mystery, book 10
Truffled Murder
A Pumpkin Hollow Mystery, book 11
Caramel Murder
A Pumpkin Hollow Mystery, book 12

Peppermint Fudge Killer
A Pumpkin Hollow Mystery, book 13
Chocolate Heart Killer
A Pumpkin Hollow Mystery, book 14
Strawberry Creams and Death
A Pumpkin Hollow Mystery, book 15
Pumpkin Spice Lies
A Pumpkin Hollow Mystery, book 16
Sweetly Dead
A Pumpkin Hollow Mystery, book 17
Deadly Valentine
A Pumpkin Hollow Mystery, book 18
Death and a Peppermint Patty
A Pumpkin Hollow Mystery, book 19
Sugar, Spice, and Murder
A Pumpkin Hollow Mystery, book 20
Candy Crushed
A Pumpkin Hollow Mystery, book 21
Trick or Treat
A Pumpkin Hollow Mystery, book 22
Frightfully Dead
A Pumpkin Hollow Mystery, book 23

A Freshly Baked Cozy Mystery Series

Apple Pie a la Murder,
A Freshly Baked Cozy Mystery, Book 1
Trick or Treat and Murder,
A Freshly Baked Cozy Mystery, Book 2
Thankfully Dead
A Freshly Baked Cozy Mystery, Book 3

Candy Cane Killer
A Freshly Baked Cozy Mystery, Book 4
Ice Cold Murder
A Freshly Baked Cozy Mystery, Book 5
Love is Murder
A Freshly Baked Cozy Mystery, Book 6
Strawberry Surprise Killer
A Freshly Baked Cozy Mystery, Book 7
Plum Dead
A Freshly Baked Cozy Mystery, book 8
Red, White, and Blue Murder
A Freshly Baked Cozy Mystery, book 9
Mummy Pie Murder
A Freshly Baked Cozy Mystery, book 10
Wedding Bell Blunders
A Freshly Baked Cozy Mystery, book 11
In a Jam
A Freshly Baked Cozy Mystery, book 12
Tarts and Terror
A Freshly Baked Cozy Mystery, book 13
Fall for Murder
A Freshly Baked Cozy Mystery, book 14
Web of Deceit
A Freshly Baked Cozy Mystery, book 15
Silenced Santa
A Freshly Baked Cozy Mystery, book 16
New Year, New Murder
A Freshly Baked Cozy Mystery, book 17
Murder Supreme

A Cookie's Creamery Mystery

A Lemon Creek Mystery

A Home Economics Mystery Series

Made in United States
North Haven, CT
29 August 2023

40898937R00093